SILVERWORLD

SILVERWORLD

Diana Abu-Jaber

CROWN BOOKS
FOR YOUNG READERS
New York

Text copyright © 2020 by Diana Abu-Jaber
Jacket art copyright © 2020 by Anoosha Syed

Visit us on the Web! rhcbooks.com

Educators and librarians, for a variety of teaching tools, visit us at RHTeachersLibrarians.com

Library of Congress Cataloging-in-Publication Data
Names: Abu-Jaber, Diana, author.
Title: Silverworld / Diana Abu-Jaber.
Description: First edition. | New York: Crown Books for Young Readers, [2020] | Audience: Ages 8–12. | Audience: Grades 4–6. | Summary: Desperate to help her ailing grandmother, Sami consults Teta's spell book and falls into the magical Silverworld, where she must try to save the enchanted city and, perhaps, Teta, too.
Identifiers: LCCN 2019030708 (print) | LCCN 2019030709 (ebook) |
ISBN 978-0-553-50967-0 (hardcover) | ISBN 978-0-553-50968-7 (library binding) |
ISBN 978-0-553-50969-4 (ebook)
Subjects: CYAC: Magic—Fiction. | Grandmothers—Fiction. | Sick—Fiction. | Lebanese Americans—Fiction. | Fantasy.
Classification: LCC PZ7.1.A19 Sil 2020 (print) | LCC PZ7.1.A19 (ebook) |
DDC [Fic]—dc23

Printed in the United States of America
10 9 8 7 6 5 4 3 2
First Edition

To Grace, who rides the moonlight

❦

I

"The moon was flat and white as a witch's face."

Teta leaned forward, her black eyes bright as she told her story.

"I could hear the hooves of the desert raiders as they crossed the sands. All the others slept soundly in their tents. I was all alone, twelve years old—the only one who knew they were coming!"

"Wasn't your mother there? Why didn't you wake her?" Sami whispered.

Teta threw out her arms dramatically: light glinted on her silver necklace and Sami caught a glimpse of one of the Bedouin tattoos that scrolled up her grandmother's arms. "I tried! But we'd led our caravan all the way to Wadi Rum that day. Miles and miles over burning sand. Everyone was exhausted and sound asleep. And these were no ordinary bandits—the raiders were horrible brutes. I knew they would take everything—every horse and goat. And worse. I'd heard the whispers that they stole children, sold them into slavery. I shook my mother. I cried out, 'The bandits are coming!' All she did was mutter and roll back to sleep. Oh, it was awful—I was so scared."

Sami leaned back on her grandmother's soft silk carpet. The smell of jasmine and wild thyme faintly reached her from the shelves that lined the bedroom. "What did you do?" Even though she'd heard the story many times before, she still felt breathless.

For a moment, Teta's lined face looked years younger, the light having shifted so her hair seemed to regain its black luster and the gray faded; she sat straighter, her neck lifting. She adjusted her sapphire ring. "I felt *her.*"

"Ashrafieh?" Sami whispered.

"My double." Teta nodded slowly. "I'd always known she existed. My great-uncle had told me of her for years. But this was the first time I'd felt her—deep in my center."

"What did she feel like?"

"Like courage. And cunning. A powerful current rising up from my center." Teta placed one hand on her solar plexus and Sami touched her own chest, somehow feeling that same hidden *something*. "And a voice. Like it came from my own smartest self. Speaking from deep inside a hidden world. She said to me: *Remember your training, Serafina. Call for an enchantment!*"

"An enchantment—from the spell book, you mean?" Sami asked eagerly. "When can I see it?"

"Are you twelve yet?" Teta's eyes widened.

"Practically! It's just a few weeks—"

"When you're *twelve*," Teta cut in. "There are so many wonderful adventures ahead of you. As well as many ... challenges," she added. There was the briefest hesitation in her voice, then she waved her hand. "Let's not rush into things."

"But I'm ready now. I've been ready for ages," Sami moaned.

"*And* you're interrupting the story." Teta shook her head. "Listen! I pushed back the tent flap—it was heavy, made of goat hair—very good for keeping out dust and noise. I always preferred sleeping under the night sky, but my mother wouldn't let me. I stood—the raiders were coming so near I could see the smoke of the horses' breath, the foam on their muzzles. I lifted my hands straight up to the stars. I was shaking, scared as a little chicken, but I'd heard my mother and great-uncle use the enchantment spell many times and I knew it by heart. I'd never spoken it out loud before, though, and I didn't know if it would work for me—the magical ordering of words and sound. Still, I shouted it out with all my might."

"And the bandits stopped," Sami said, grinning.

Teta nodded. "Maybe twenty meters away. The ones who were jumping off their horses just flopped to the ground. Others fell asleep while they were still up on their horses. Their headscarves unwinding, all their gold teeth showing. They were dreadful, these monsters with their daggers drawn."

"And their horses fell asleep too."

"Yes," Teta said with a wide smile. "I hadn't learned my own magicking strength yet. I didn't know how to control my spell

3

casting. By then my great-uncle Kashmir had risen—he was still wrapping his headscarf over his hair. He ran out, looked at the fallen raiders, and said, '*Ya Allah*, child, you have the touch of the *Ifrit*!'"

The *Ifrit*. Sami shivered with delight. *Ifrit* were magical sprites—sometimes called fairies, mermaids, angels, genies—that Teta said you could summon through dreams and visions and spells. They were creatures from the Other Worlds—places that Teta hinted at and promised to tell her about . . . someday. Always another day. "Did you tell him? Did he know about your guide, Ashrafieh?" Sami rolled forward onto her knees, the question urgent.

"Ashrafieh was a Flicker, not an *Ifrit*," Teta reminded Sami.

"What's the difference again?"

"Oh, the *Ifrit* serve no one, and they create as many problems as they solve! But a *Flicker*? Well now . . ."

But before Teta could say another word, the bedroom door swung open.

2

"Serafina? Oh dear. Will you look at that plate. *Why* aren't you eating your eggs?" Aunt Ivory came into the bedroom, followed closely by Sami's mother, Alia. Ivory pointed her long nose at the plate full of cold scrambled eggs on Teta's nightstand. "Your daughter made them special—just the way you like them."

For the past two years, Teta had eaten all her meals in her room and mostly refused to leave, except when her daughter dragged her out to the doctor. Easing back in her corner chair under the reading light, Teta said a few words to Alia in her nonsense language. Sami gritted her teeth in frustration. Why did her grandmother have to make things so much harder on herself?

Alia sighed and gave her sister-in-law an apologetic look. "She had a bad night," Alia said. "I could hear her tossing and moaning. When I got up to check on her, she'd fallen back asleep."

"It's completely understandable." Ivory lifted her eyebrows. "These sorts of things happen more often as we get older."

These sorts of things. Leaning against the heavy wardrobe, Sami sighed deeply. She knew what her aunt was referring to—the fact that Teta didn't seem to know how to speak clearly anymore. A year ago—actually, longer—Sami's grandmother, her teta, had stopped talking. Well, she *talked*—she just didn't use words that other people could understand. It happened slowly. First there would be one or two of these strange words that sort of popped up as she spoke. If you asked Teta what this or that meant, she would frown like you were being difficult and just keep talking. Over time, though, the nonsense words started to drown out the regular words. Sami used to beg her, "Why are you doing that? Can't you just talk regular?"

The really weird part was that when they were alone, just the two of them in the room, Teta spoke perfectly clearly. No impossible words or nonsense. Sami told her mother, her brother, even her slightly horrible aunt, but none of them believed her. They said that was ridiculous—how could anyone deliberately keep up an act like that for so long? Sami couldn't even understand it herself. All she knew was that whenever she asked Teta about the nonsense words, she didn't seem to know what Sami was talking about. "I talk just fine," she said indignantly. "It's the others with a problem!"

Ivory bustled around Teta and picked up the plate of eggs.

To Sami's dismay, her aunt speared some eggs on a fork and held them up to Teta's face. "Come now, dear, just a bite. For me."

Teta made a big annoyed, abrupt gesture with her hands, as if she wanted to sweep Ivory out the door, but the back of Teta's hand accidentally hit the plate of eggs and sent them flying.

"Agh!" Ivory flinched. There was egg speckled all over the front of her silk blouse.

"*Mother*," Alia snapped. She rushed to Ivory. "I'm so sorry! Oh, your beautiful blouse. Come, come—let's see if we can't get that out. . . ."

The two women hurried away, leaving Sami and her grandmother. Teta's palms were pressed to the sides of her face. Her round black eyes turned to Sami. "Sseb-ssebb," she garbled. "Aaal . . . feeek farab aam. . . ."

"It's okay, Teta." Sami crouched beside her grandmother and started picking up bits of egg. "It was an accident. They know you didn't mean it." *At least*, she thought, *I hope they do.* It broke Sami's heart to see Teta looking hurt and upset. *That's what it feels like to not be able to defend yourself.*

"Truly, just a stupid—a mistake. . . ." Teta stared at the door, returning to normal language again. "So clumsy."

"But, um, Teta?" Sami interrupted. "Seriously, you do have to eat *something*. I mean, I think Mom's starting to get, like, worried about you and all." A couple of months ago, she had noticed that her grandmother was eating less and less of the food they brought to her room. Sami tried to cover for her, taking a few extra bites before she returned the dishes to the kitchen, where her mother would sigh over them. But lately, Teta was eating so little that there was no disguising it—she looked thin and frail. And now Aunt Ivory had to get right into the middle of things. She'd started talking about sending Teta out to an old folks' home ever since they'd gotten to Florida. Sami remembered the sour lemon expression on her aunt's face as she brushed off egg crumbs.

Teta hummed and looked away in that aggravating I-don't-want-to-talk-about-it way of hers—like Sami was the seventy-year-old and Teta was the one about to turn twelve. Sami sighed and placed the plate of spilled eggs on the nightstand. Voices reached her from downstairs. Through the walls, she could hear a sound of water rushing, maybe arguing? Then a door slammed.

"If you would just—talk normally to them!" Sami pleaded with her grandmother for the hundredth time. "They think you're losing it, Teta."

Ten minutes ago, Teta's eyes had flashed with daring as she recalled her nights in the desert. Now her face looked pinched and white. Terrified. And at that moment, Sami had the weirdest, most chilling sensation—the feeling that Teta *didn't* speak any differently when she was with her granddaughter, that she spoke the same way to Sami that she did with everyone else. Maybe Sami wasn't *supposed* to be able to understand her grandmother any more than anyone else did. And yet for some reason she did.

With this thought in her head, she jumped up from the floor. "Excuse me, Teta, I've gotta go talk to Mom for a second."

She felt her grandmother's eyes on her, as if Teta wanted—needed—to tell her something. And yet lately it seemed harder and harder for Teta to tell even her stories. Her memory seemed increasingly misty and her handwriting had turned into an indecipherable series of scratches and dashes. Still, even though Teta had lapsed into silence, Sami could see some urgent, unspoken thought, right there on her grandmother's face. And she knew Teta would open up only when she was good and ready to.

3

Sami went down the stairs cautiously, looking over both shoulders for her aunt, but there was no sign of Ivory. She found her mother sitting alone at the dining room table, her head in her hands. Alia looked up with a soft smile. "Hi, honey. Aunt Ivory went home. Um, to clean up."

"Teta totally didn't mean to do that, Mom. It was just a dumb accident. You know that."

"Oh, I know. It's too bad it was such a . . . messy one." She laughed sadly.

Sami sensed there was something else that her mother wanted to say—something that she didn't want to hear—but Alia was going to try to pretend that there wasn't. "Hey, let's think about your birthday plans," her mom said, straightening up. "What do you say—let's go up to Disney! You, me, and Tony. We've never gone—it'll be fun!"

"You're forgetting someone," Sami said.

"Well . . . we really couldn't take your grandmother along," Alia said in a gentle voice. "She's just—she's unsteady—these days."

Sami shook her head. "Teta is fine. She's being weird about some stuff right now. But basically she's really, really fine."

Alia took a deep breath. In the silence, Sami could hear the soft *tick, tick, tick* of her brother's basketball bouncing in the driveway, the scuffle of his feet. "Sami. We need to talk."

Sami sighed as quietly as she could.

Alia went on: "Your grandmother—she isn't fine, honey. When people get older, sometimes they start to have problems. They get frail, they can't think clearly."

"But she isn't like that. I know, I know—she's doing this weird thing with the way she talks. But you have to listen. When Teta and I are alone? She talks completely normally!"

Alia held her hands open. "Sami, if your grandmother has been speaking nonsense to me and the entire world—everyone but you—for over a year—is that behaving normally?"

Sami's eyes prickled with tears; she gritted her teeth, refusing to cry. She didn't know how to explain things to her mother so she'd understand. She barely understood it herself.

"I'd like to show you something." Alia was already standing, removing an envelope from a stack of papers on the kitchen counter. She returned to the table and placed a brochure in front of Sami. It had a picture of a smiling white-haired woman with a nurse standing behind her, and said SILVER BEACHES MANOR. "Your aunt Ivory and I have been talking quite a bit and—well—sweetie—we both feel like Teta is starting to need more help. More than we can give her at home."

"So you just want to, what? Stick her in one of those places? Where you don't have to think about her?"

"Sami." Now her mother was using her attorney voice. "This is about what's best for *Teta*. She's losing weight; she's becoming a shut-in. I don't like this any better than you do. In assisted care she'll be able to socialize more, get therapy. They're doing amazing things with dementia patients. . . ."

"Dementia?" Sami shook her head. "Teta doesn't have dementia!" She kept her voice lowered, worried her grandmother would hear them, but she couldn't help the tears that started to well up. "Why do you even listen to Aunt Ivory so much, anyway? Just because she's Dad's sister. Sometimes I think you care more about what she thinks than what Tony or I do."

"Samara, you know that's not true," Alia said sternly.

"I don't know anything!" Sami wailed, and ran out of the room.

4

Sami sat on the front steps with her chin in her hands and watched her big brother shoot hoops.

Overhead, the sky was a dazzling, watercolor blue, criss-crossed with squawking parrots, palm fronds, and golden hibiscus flowers. It was just as weird here, she sometimes thought, as in her dreams. Before they'd moved, she'd never imagined a place like Coconut Shores even existed. She was used to cold lakes and old mountains and fireplaces. They'd been here nearly a year, and while she could *see* how pretty Florida was, she often thought she couldn't feel it. Not deep down. And why should she? Whenever her mom put on the news, it was all about global warming and how Florida was about to be underwater. Or pollution and toxic algae. Or deadly mosquitoes, or people on drugs. Every day things just seemed to get worse and worse—

lately, she'd had the feeling that the whole world was getting out of balance, somehow. But no one wanted to see it. People acted like all that mattered was the blue sky and the beach.

Tony had waved to her when she came out, but kept dribbling, his hair spiky with sweat—six days past Thanksgiving and still eighty degrees out. Sami pulled her knees up and rested her chin on top of them, eternally grateful that her brother didn't mind having a kid sister. He had a big, easy smile and a good loose laugh, and there had seemed to be a crowd of teenagers over at the house practically the second they moved in. Sami still didn't have any real *friend*-friends here. Not like Tony. Instead, she sent texts to her old friends in Ithaca, about the dumb Coconut Shores girls who only cared about their tans and makeup.

"Hey, kiddo." Tony came over, rubbing the back of his neck with a towel. He was just three years older than Sami and it used to be funny when he called her that. Lately, though, it kind of bothered her. "You okay?"

Sami lowered her face, annoyed. She'd never learned how to control her own facial expressions very well. *You must learn how to put on your veil*, her grandmother had said, fanning out a hand over her mouth and nose like a belly dancer. "When you need to."

"Aunt Ivory was bugging Teta again." She handed a thermos of clinking ice water to her brother.

"Hey! Thanks." He gulped it down, then ran the length of his forearm across his brow.

"I'll never get why Mom moved us three blocks away from her. She doesn't even *like* Aunt Ivory that much; it's totally obvious," Sami groused.

Tony sat next to her on the cement steps. He shrugged. "Ivory's *family*, Sami. You can't take things so seriously—you'll go nuts."

"I've already gone."

Tony grinned. "Your words, my friend, your words."

"So, guess what? You know how Ivory's been wanting to stick Teta in a nursing home? Well, Mom was going on about it just now like *she's* starting to have the same idea. It was horrible. I wouldn't let her even talk about it."

Tony's eyebrows rose. Their mother was a defense attorney, famous in their family for never backing off in an argument. "How'd you stop her? From talking about it, I mean."

Sami took a sip from her own thermos. "I basically ran out."

He nodded heavily. "That works, I guess. It's not like she isn't going to keep talking about it nonstop, anyway."

Sami sighed, her face against her knees. Then she looked at Tony, frowning. "So, wait—Mom already talked to you about it? About Teta?"

Tony jerked and turned away. "Uh . . ."

"And . . . you didn't say anything to me?" She frowned at her brother. "Whoa. Hold on. She's already *decided*, hasn't she? She just wanted to 'talk' so she could tell me what's going to happen. That's it, isn't it? Why didn't you warn me?"

"Jeez, Sam." Tony glanced at the basketball. There was a

deep V between his eyebrows. "Sometimes there's just no way to talk to you about stuff—you figure things out before I even know what I want to say."

"But this is *Teta* we're talking about! It's not like *Tumble*."

A few weeks after their mother had put the house on the market, Sami and Tony came home to discover that not only were they moving to Florida, but their mother had given their dog away. She'd done it without saying a word beforehand. "He'd be miserable down there in that heat—all that fur," Alia had pleaded. "And it's just too much—to try to move an old dog like that. It isn't fair to Tumble."

"What about to *us*?" Sami had cried, tears streaking her face. It was one of the few times in her life Alia had done something huge that Sami hadn't been able to sense coming. She'd never imagined such a thing. As bad as the move was, losing their dog was even worse.

Now Tony's face turned red. He was still upset about it, Sami knew. "Sami, I *know* this isn't like Tumble." His voice was stiff and strange—a deep sort of grown-uppy voice he'd started to have lately. Sometimes he almost sounded like a sad version of their father—at least of how Sami remembered him sounding. "But did you ever consider that—well, what if Mom and Aunt Ivory are actually right? I mean, Teta doesn't even make sense anymore—she's not acting normally—no matter what you say. Maybe it's not really that important how *you* feel about it. Believe it or not, maybe this is more about what's best for Teta."

Sami stood up then. Even though Tony was nearly a foot

taller than her, she glared into his eyes, anger making her whole body hot. "She doesn't have dementia now, Tony. But if we stick her in one of those places, she really will get messed up."

Tony shook his head. "This isn't like one of Teta's fairy stories. I know you think you can get inside her brain and see her hiding in there—or something. But you can't. That isn't the way this stuff works, Sami. She needs professional care and stuff. Doctors. Not make-believe."

Sami pulled back. She'd never before heard Tony make fun of Teta's stories—real or not. She glared at him for a second before she said in a low voice, "You're not one of the grown-ups, Tony. Not yet, anyway. And I wish you'd quit trying to be. I wish you'd just—like—be a *kid* again. Or my brother. The way you used to be!"

Tony shook his head and dribbled toward the basketball hoop, saying as he went, "Yeah, and I wish *you'd* try growing up."

5

The house was quiet and empty when Sami went back inside. A note on the kitchen table said that her mother had taken Teta to a doctor's appointment. It didn't matter, Sami thought despondently. She just wanted to hide in her room, anyway. There, she pouted at her mirror, scowled fiercely, hands on her hips.

After a moment, her shoulders lowered and she plopped on her bed. Tilted against the wall and framed by a frill of silver waves, the mirror gazed back at her. Its glass was so old, it looked blue and weathered in long strips across its surface. Teta said it was created by mermaids, before the creation of glass itself, and had been handed down through the family from an *Ifrit*, courageous Magali of Palmyra—that it was an enchanted mirror, a doorway to other lands. And, Teta always added, it must never, under any circumstances, ever be covered up.

"They brought it for me on an airplane," Teta had said, lifting her knobby hands in the air. "All the way from Lebanon. Three strong men carried it in a big crate right up to our house." She smiled. In those days, her teeth were magically white, her skin still smooth. "That was your father's idea. Joe knew how much it meant to me. He found a way to save it."

A couple of years after Joe died, Teta told Sami she wanted her to have it. "When you miss him, you look right here." She'd pointed to the silver surface. "You can talk to him and he will hear you."

Sami was only six at the time, but she had still wondered how her daddy could be in the mirror. She kept thinking: *He's just gone.*

Teta had hugged her and said, "Think of it as a window. He's not *in* the glass, but you can speak through it to wherever he is."

Now Sami glanced at herself in the mirror. Did her face seem brighter? Was there an unusual sort of gleam on her skin and hair? She slid off her bed, crouched next to the mirror, and whispered to her grandmother's double, "Ashrafieh, why can't I have someone like you? Someone who would make me strong or smart or something?"

For a moment, out of the corner of her eye, she seemed to see reflected blue dots twinkling in the air. But they vanished as soon as she turned. Sami closed her eyes and shook her head, trying to clear out all the shadows and cobwebs. *Seeing things.* Teta often talked about spells and trances, people who were haunted by genies. She knew all the ways someone could be inhabited or spellbound. Born into a Bedouin tribe, Teta said she had sand and sunlight in her blood, that she'd been a desert dweller for many, many lifetimes. She wore a necklace of silver coins and told her grandchildren that she'd grown up crossing the desert, learning about potions and herbs.

But then everything changed. The magic stopped. A handsome man from Beirut had won her heart and moved her to his house. Her daughter, Alia, was raised in the city, and then Teta's grandchildren were all the way Americans. Sometimes it seemed as if Teta was still back there, crossing the desert in her mind, living among the Bedouin legends and charms, while the rest of the world had moved on. In fact, Sami wasn't always sure if her wonderful grandmother really was still entirely there— inside her body, still the Teta she had always known. She'd gotten shrunken, secretive, her eyes full of a mysterious fear.

Worrying, Sami felt her own breath catch in her throat. She looked up again at the mirror and this time she felt distinctly as if her reflection was gazing at her. It wasn't just the reflection of her eyes, but more as if there was someone else inside there, *looking back*. That's when she had a new idea: what if *Teta* believed she was under one of those Bedouin spells? There were the princesses mesmerized by their own reflections in gazing pools, young sailors who fell under the whispered incantations of mermaids, entire families lost and wandering in the wilderness of the genies.

Sami got slowly to her feet. She didn't necessarily believe in magic, but Teta surely did. What was that old quote her grandmother loved? *There is far more unseen than seen in the natural world.* And hadn't they learned in health class just last week that a person could make themselves sick simply by thinking they were sick? *Psychosomatic*, the teacher had written on the whiteboard. It was sort of a weird idea, but maybe, she thought . . . just maybe . . . Sami could convince Teta that she knew how to break the hex.

She put her hands on her hips, thinking and pacing. If there was one thing she knew for certain—Teta's charm book was the one source of all things enchanted. Sami had to find it. It was an old book with a cracked leather cover that Teta had brought with her from Lebanon. She told people it was just a diary. But she'd admitted to Sami, with a finger to her lips, that it was really a book of great and magical powers. She kept it hidden away, and she had instructed Sami that she must never touch or even look at it if Teta wasn't with her. Teta promised that once Sami turned twelve, she'd begin revealing the book's secrets to her. But her birthday was still weeks away, and judging by her mother's determined expression, Sami sensed there was no time to spare: Sami would have to search for the book. And she would have to do it quickly.

6

Back in their house in Ithaca, the book's hiding place used to be under her grandmother's pillow. But now, sliding her hand under the thin, jasmine-scented pillow, Sami found only prayer beads. Luckily, Teta didn't have a lot of furniture or possessions, so the hiding places were limited. Sami moved quickly and carefully, trying not to leave any trace of her hunt. She looked behind the painting of the Virgin Mary—which Teta sometimes called "Fatima" and sometimes "The Goddess"—hanging over the bed. She rummaged through colored jars of myrrh and sandalwood oil and other murky potions on Teta's dresser, green and amber and sea-colored glass jars labeled in smudged Arabic. A single clear vial said MAGICK WATER. In the closet that Teta liked to call her "memory cabinet," there were olive oil soaps, Teta's fortune-telling cards, ointments from the Dead Sea, a whittled caravan of camels linked by silver chains. But no spell book.

Bookshelves? Check. Bed stand? Check. Under her rocker, her floor lamp, her jewelry box? Check, check, and check. Sami stood in the middle of the room, frowning, hands on her hips. She hadn't seen the old book in a long time—certainly not since they'd moved. Yet Teta *had* to still have it. The book was as prized as the mirror, possibly more so. That was, she supposed, why her grandmother hid it so well. Too darn well.

She looked at Teta's little table clock with the Indian numbers and the bent hands that seemed to move backward. Teta and her mother had been gone for over an hour and could be back at any time.

Under the bed, she was startled to discover a half-filled suitcase. Perhaps this was just extra storage, she tried to reassure herself. Perhaps Teta had packed it herself, planning a trip? Not likely. These were all of Teta's clothes, folded in her mother's neat piles. They were already getting her ready to go, Sami thought darkly. Maybe Alia was even planning to move Teta this week.

Never.

Sami couldn't accept that. She would not. Her father used to tell her, *Don't you ever give up on anything important, Sami.* It hardly even mattered how things turned out—just as long as you tried your hardest and never quit. It was a feeling she'd sensed inside herself for nearly all her life—especially when her teta told her stories of the ancient beings, the *Ifrit*, and the Flickers who stood up against demons. She felt it when she heard about the ruined castles and giantess princesses, women generals and warriors her grandmother was descended from.

Sami folded her arms tightly, which had always been her

best thinking position. It felt like she could pull the energy from her heart right into her mind that way. She took a couple of deep breaths, looked back at Teta's pillow—the place the spell book should have been—and tried to clear her mind.

A glimmer started to tickle the back of her thoughts. She blinked at the door and the hallway beyond. Slowly, Sami went out and walked back to her own room. She looked in her closet—almost as orderly as Teta's. Sami kept things so neat, it was hard to imagine anything stashed in her room that she wouldn't notice immediately. Still, a little premonition, like an itch between the shoulder blades, kept her looking. She poked through her desk and dresser, all around her bed, under the mattress. She pushed aside stacks of textbooks for school, the unstarted project for social studies class, pre-algebra homework—then she looked under the bed. Their new Florida house had so few closets, Alia stored odds and ends down there—Christmas decorations, some cleaning supplies, a stack of her old *Law Review* journals, and a small rolled-up carpet. Sami was about to stand, then thought better of it, and reached over and pulled out the carpet. It was the kind that Muslims knelt on to say their prayers. When Teta and her daughter immigrated to the States, Teta had brought one small suitcase and the prayer rug on the plane. She said she liked to "pick and choose" her beliefs, and frequently mentioned that she had her own private faith. Even so, the rug was a rare and beautiful memento of her Bedouin childhood—an item, like the mirror, that had been handed down through her tribe. As a little girl,

Sami had liked to run her hands over its silk threads, vibrant whorls of blue and red, and pretend she was on a flying carpet.

The rolled carpet was held in place with a piece of twine. She unknotted it and opened the carpet, and the scent of lemon, sand, and sunlight filled the air.

Lying in the center of the carpet was the spell book.

Sami sat back on her heels, breathless.

She admired her grandmother's forethought. Teta had probably guessed her daughter was planning to do something drastic—maybe even send her away—and decided to hide the book here for safekeeping. It was slightly curved from being rolled up, and its leather cover was battered and worn, but it was in surprisingly good shape, Sami thought, for something that looked about a zillion years old.

She ran her fingers over the book's nubbly surface, then carefully turned the gleaming, gilt-edged pages. The paper was so thin, it barely made a wisp of a sound as she leafed through. There were diagrams and drawings of things that looked like mysterious inventions, with arrows and circles and dotted lines, but whenever she tried to look closely at an illustration, it seemed to shift slightly out of focus. A light herbal scent of flowers, lilacs and geraniums—and different sorts of unidentifiable fruits and spices—seemed to waft up as she turned the pages, then vanish just as quickly. Everything was written in thin black pen strokes, a flowing, perfect penmanship. Again, Sami ran her finger along the pen's faint indentations—nothing like her grandmother's handwriting—and tried to read, but almost none of it was written in English. She thought she could recognize bits of French and Arabic. At least she thought it might be, as these letters, too, seemed to slightly bounce and jiggle whenever she tried to look directly at them.

It was almost like the book was trying to avoid her. Like the book itself was under a spell.

She smirked and rolled her eyes at herself, but kept turning the slippery pages. Twice, wisps of things—tiny feathers or petals—tumbled from the book, but when Sami bent to retrieve them, they winked out before she could touch them. The book was so old and delicate, she felt like a clumsy oaf trying to thumb through a fairy's storybook. She paged faster, aware of precious minutes slipping by, her frustration building. Finally, she was about to give up on the book when she came to a page where the writing stood precisely still.

The words looked like some sort of incantation, written partially in gibberish. Directly underneath the first line of garbled words, in small faint letters, it said:

Thee Opfening of thee Silverskinn'd

Beside this was an ink drawing of a mirror. The same mirror, to be exact, that stood in Sami's room. There were the same waves and swirls that framed the long rectangle—even the dented glass in the middle. She realized then she could make out in the drawing the faint image of a face in the mirror . . . which looked oddly like Sami's—it had the same round black eyes and curling black hair. She shivered a bit, then tried to laugh at herself. It was just a drawing!

There was something about the scrambled language that looked familiar as well—*kkeeff karaaaab yyallu: ahtttah li rraaad il raamsim.*

Sami climbed back on her bed and looked up at her reflection in the mirror again. The words reminded her of Teta's jumbled language. It was just as if the book itself had taken her to this page. Her breath sped up and her eyes grew wide: it seemed almost possible she was holding the key to her grandmother's cure right there in her hands. But did she dare to try a spell? Her grandmother always emphasized the powerful— and unpredictable—nature of enchantments. For some reason, one of her mother's favorite expressions popped into her head: *The only way out is through.* It was something Alia would say when she was tackling a tough case or a mountain of briefs and paperwork.

Just outside came the sound of a car door closing.

Sami jumped and almost dropped the book. There was no time to waste. She didn't know exactly what this spell was supposed to do, only that the book itself had nearly placed these words in her lap. Sami stood and held the old thing up carefully before her. She was just a few feet from her mirror and could see all of herself reflected in it. Her reflection looked frightened and unsure, but also maybe even a little bit brave. Yes. Determined. She hoped her own secret strength was there too, like her grandmother's Ashrafieh, trying to unfold.

"Mother! What's the matter now?" Alia's voice came through the window from their driveway. "Easy, easy. Please, calm yourself. I'll have you back upstairs in just a minute."

There was a long, agitated string of Teta's strange words.

"Why are you being like this? *Shoo, habibti?* Just take it easy, I'm coming around to your side now—I'll let you right out. . . ."

She knows I have the book, Sami thought in a panic. Somehow, *Teta knows!*

The tiny words ran under the unknown lines like a kind of translation. Squinting, heart hammering in her chest, Sami began to read aloud: *"Beautifull Silverskinn'd, greatest door to Worldes beside Worldes beside Worldes, please to hear mine enjoindre. I heare the Friende and I Respond. O, Silverskinn'd, parte your Gaetes and admit me. . . ."*

There was the sound of a second car door closing. She read faster:

"I atteste that I am Capable and Authorize'd, and that I am One of the Treu Silverwalkers, read'eed to pass threuw the Gaetes. For this Favore I grant You mine Favore, which is Luve and Obeisance. Threuw the Gaetes I go Willinglee and Joyeouslee, knowing once threuw, nevermore I may retourn Un-change'ed."

Sami lowered the book then. Her face in the mirror looked ashen, her heart was pounding, and for some reason she was completely out of breath, panting like she'd run a mile, but nothing else was happening. For a moment, she felt a kind of terrified uncertainty: this *had* to work! It would be unbearable to step back from whatever brink this was. It would not only fail Teta, but also prove her grandmother was wrong—about many things—especially and worst of all about the magical worlds.

Through her anxiety, Sami realized her head seemed to be swimming with a dense murk: she heard and felt things as if they were coming to her from a great distance. She turned toward the front door. It was opening, but the sound itself seemed to come from far away. Was she dreaming?

She closed the book, and was sliding it under her blankets when she noticed a soft blue light cast over her bed. She blinked. All along its edges, in each corner, the mirror had started to glow.

She blinked several more times, bit the inside of her cheek, pinched her arm and felt it sharply.

This was not a dream.

At the center of the mirror a dot expanded into a white beam: it grew and cut through her room, sweeping across Sami's body. She felt shimmering under her skin. It was a wondrous, silky, free-flying sensation. It felt like being born and swimming in a warm pool and climbing the highest tree and eating chocolate ice cream, and having her mother and father and grandparents and brother wrap their arms around her all at the same time.

No matter what happens, Sami thought, *whether Teta gets well or gets sent away or I get into a million years of trouble or I'm grounded forever, no matter what—this feeling, right now, makes everything worth it.*

She closed her eyes and took a deep, sweet breath, wishing she could have this feeling forever, and that's when she felt the floor disappear from under her feet.

7

She plunged.

Her feet flew over her head, her arms were thrown open, then her head was over her feet, then down again. It was like being tumbled in the most enormous waves: a roar from underneath the planet swept her body and she felt rushing and frothing. Her eyes filled with blue light, light seemed to be pouring from her ears and mouth and fingertips, and there was no time to scream or breathe, only to twist and spin.

And then not.

Light sucked inside out and everything was gone—no color, no shades, no dimension. No Sami. All was flat and nothing. It was just a blink. Like existence held its breath. Then released.

And light—in all delicate gradients and hues and colors— rolled back in.

Now she drifted. As if she were made of feathers. One great feather. Gently, gently lowering, rocking, lowering, at last settling into stillness. She sank into something with the softness of feathers, water, air.

Easing deeper. Into sleep.

ᔕᔑ

There were voices. No. It was only one voice. And there was that good feeling again. Not as strong as before. Where was she now? Her eyes were closed and she seemed to be riding a little cushion of air. It rose and fell very gently with each of her breaths, like a cradle made from a cloud.

There was a sweet, rocking sensation inside her body and mind, tipping one way, then the other, gentle and satisfying, as if she herself had become the cradle. Something—or someone—was stroking her hands.

The voice blurred slightly. She couldn't quite focus enough in order to hear. Words coming together:

Alive . . . you . . .
Like . . . seeing . . . wanted . . . dense.
Friend . . . waken . . .

She struggled to open her eyes. Her eyelids felt heavy, as if there were tiny weights attached to them. She began to crack them open, but sharp blue-and-white light cut into her eyes and she flinched, squeezing them shut.

"No, your eyes! Wait, Sami!" the voice cried. She realized then that the first words she'd heard hadn't been spoken aloud, yet somehow she'd still managed to hear them. She felt hands on her head—the feeling that something was sliding over her face. "Okay—yes. Now, gently, Sami. Open slowly."

She lifted her eyes slowly and this time the intense colors were softer. She could just make out a shadowy head hovering over her.

"You're not used yet to our light," the voice said. "It will take some minutes at least."

Sami realized that this creature or person standing before her was where the good feeling had come from. As she gazed at it, she started to remember what had happened: how she'd stood before the mirror with her grandmother's spell book, reading those words, then fell forward into the mirror as this lovely, sweet sensation swept over her. The feeling was little more than a faint echo now. She squinted through bands of color and light and began to make out more details. The speaker appeared to be a boy, several years older than Sami, with round black eyes, green skin, and long, waving deep-black hair. He wore a checked scarf around his shoulders that reminded her of the headscarves men wore in Lebanon. He seemed intensely familiar to her, like a long-lost best friend, like someone she'd known all her life—and yet she was pretty sure she'd never seen him before. "You look like me," she said hazily, her voice thick and slow. "Are you—like—a dream?"

His smile was wide and bright. "I am Dorsom. I'm sure I must seem very like dreams to you now. But no. I'm a Flicker. We are—well, how to say it so you understand? We're reflections. Sort of." Dorsom didn't have an accent, but the slightly clipped way he talked reminded her of how some of the people in her family spoke English.

"Reflections . . ." She looked around, carefully sitting up. "Is this place—are we—inside the mirror somehow?"

Dorsom stared at her, blinking, and she felt a hum of surprise that seemed to come directly from him.

Now she sat a bit straighter, carefully balancing. Her body felt somehow featherlight. She attempted to pull her thoughts together. "Are we still—in the world?"

"It's a world of a *kind*," Dorsom said. She noticed his eyes flick away and back again. He seemed preoccupied or distracted. "We're in Silverworld, Sami. The World next door."

"And *that*—how do you know my name?" Sami pushed back her elbows.

"Take care," Dorsom said. "You're not used to our air yet."

"I'm not used to . . . what?" Sami tried to stand up and nearly fell right back over. She was solid, yet couldn't feel the weight of her own body. Her head spun for a second and her ears fizzed. "Whoa!" She braced against the ground, her hand brushing silky golden weeds. She realized she and the boy were out in some sort of open field—red stones and sandy bramble.

Gradually, her sense of balance began to return. "What on earth is going on? What's wrong with me?"

But he didn't answer. Instead, he shifted into a squat, eyes scanning all around. Sami followed his gaze and saw that the field was bordered on one side by a row of distant houses. She squinted, tilting her head; the perspective changed and the houses looked much closer and quite familiar.

"I'm—I'm at home! We're not in another world, we're in my backyard." She marveled, gazing around at scrubby weeds and sand, noticing bands of soft colors—the weeds lavender and the palm trees rippling coral red. "Only, well . . . it's not totally my backyard. . . ."

Then something like a surge or pulse ran through the air. Sami couldn't see or hear it but she felt it clearly. "Oh! Wow."

"What is it?" he asked. "What do you feel?"

She stared at Dorsom, still shocked and afraid, yet she had the strongest sense that this was someone she could trust. His warm black eyes were so familiar, it was somehow as if they were old friends who'd never met before.

He stood. "You must have picked up on something. It wouldn't take long, I knew. Best we get going."

"Going?" Sami wasn't sure she could even get to her feet, but he took her hand and she rose effortlessly. "My gosh!" She started to laugh but then she felt the pulse through the air again—this time deeper and stronger, like a shock wave. It was as if, for an instant, everything had turned into ripples on a pond.

He asked, *Is something coming?*

Sami nodded, though she wasn't sure how she knew. Then she realized again he hadn't spoken the words out loud. "Wait. How are you—?"

Walking swiftly, Dorsom beckoned, and with his thoughts he called, *Let us go now. Most quickly. Let's go.*

8

Sami still wasn't sure what was happening here, but the intensifying, increasing pulse in the air made her feel as if her very bones had turned cold. "Wait! Wait for me!"

Catching up to Dorsom, Sami asked, "Where are we going?" They were walking swiftly and it almost felt more like flying. She barely felt the ground under her feet. They dodged around the back of a house very similar to the one she lived in—except this one had a soft orange glow. Sami started to turn toward it, but Dorsom said, "No. This isn't the Actual World, Sami. It's not your World."

"What—where are—?" Sami didn't even know which question to ask first.

He muttered with his thoughts, *Please. For now—just keep going.* They walked past houses that looked vaguely like Sami's neighbors' homes, but these glowed in tones of amber, sea green, and bronze.

"Wow!" Sami gasped, her head swiveling to take in all the colors. "Just wow, wow, wow. It's beautiful."

Once they'd covered several blocks, Dorsom slowed his pace. "Don't look forth or back," he said evenly. "Better to blend right in."

Sami recognized the Flamingo Road neighborhood, and yet, like the backyard, it didn't look right. The colors were too bright and unusual; there was little grass, just expanses of sandy pink rock and scrub. The street was narrow, coral-tinted cobblestone. She seemed to hear a faint jingling in the palm fronds, and a flock of glowing fuchsia birds passing overhead seemed to be murmuring to each other in some sort of language. Was her mother or brother seeing any of this? She didn't have her phone or tablet; she wished desperately she could ask her family what was going on.

Dorsom gestured and they turned into a crowded street. Flickers strolled by, the way people did on Flamingo Road, but here they were dressed in long robes—women mostly in crimson and lemon yellow, the men in rich browns. Some wore headdresses, turbans or sand-colored headscarves. A few wore russet beads wound around their heads or their necks. There were no cars, but several Flickers walked past, leading goats or a line of sheep. One rode on a grunting, soft-eyed magenta camel. Instead of a sleepy beach town in South Florida, it all looked more like some bustling, Technicolor, Middle Eastern desert oasis, straight from one of Teta's stories.

Sami tried not to stare but she noticed a few of the Flickers glancing at her. She had the weird sense that she was being scanned somehow—and that it wasn't quite a polite thing to do either. In response, she felt herself doing something instinctive that was like sealing herself off; instantly the other Flickers looked away. She frowned, unnerved.

Well done, Dorsom said—or rather, thought—startling her again.

I didn't realize I did anything, she tried thinking back to him. *I don't even know how we're having this—conversation.*

They all assume you are a Flicker, like me. He smiled. *For an Actual person, that's some excellent reflecting you're doing.*

They walked quickly, Sami panting and struggling a bit to keep her balance on the broken, uneven cobblestones. At last they turned into a place that in Sami's World was called the Tropi Café—a squat, whitewashed stone structure with a flat roof. In this World, the sign out front had a bright chartreuse light, making it too blurry to read. They knocked, and the door opened. Dorsom led her to a table in the corner.

"This is good," Dorsom said softly as they sat. "Most Shadows dislike going indoors. We should be all right for a bit."

"We're running from *shadows?*" Sami asked, incredulous. "But why? Please, you have to tell me what is going on. I can't— I won't go any farther until I know what's happening."

A young woman closed the front door, then hurried to their table and smiled at them. "Rebalancers, welcome!" Her narrow eyes had a pewter tint and her hair glowed down her back like a sheet of cream-colored satin. She wore flat silver sandals and billowing, filmy trousers tied around her ankles with silver threads. A row of bangles clinked on her wrist. She seemed to Sami almost too beautiful to be real. "We are honored that you are amidst. May I bring you trays from our chef?"

Dorsom shook his head. "Something simple, please. Tea, bread." He looked at Sami. "The soup here is excellent."

Sami hesitated, wondered if she should ask what sort of soup it was, and then nodded. "Okay, uh, soup for me too, please."

The waitress bowed politely, backing away.

"Marvelous!" Dorsom said. "Not one discerns that you are an Actual."

"Is that good?" Sami asked, glancing at the server, who was opening the elaborate lock on the door. "What would happen if other Flickers found out about me?"

"To say is difficult." Dorsom raised his eyebrows. "I've not seen this sort of situation before. I mean, for an Actual person to Cross Over into our World. And there is less . . . tolerance . . . these days for new sorts of persons and ways of being and such."

"Everyone is upset and anxious because of all the increasing Shadow soldiers," a new voice said. Sami turned to see a woman standing near her chair. The waitress bowed and once again locked the door.

"You arrived!" Dorsom pulled out a chair, which she folded into gracefully.

The young woman had long purplish-black hair and deep

indigo skin. There were silver tattoos covering the backs of her hands, a delicate line of dots from her lower lip to her chin, and a line of silver dots above each purple eyebrow. *I heard your thoughts and rushed over here.* She turned to Sami. "It's recorded within *The Book of Silver* that in ages past, Flickers and Actuals used to regularly Cross into and out of each other's Worlds. But I never believed I would ever see someone from the Actual World in *person*." She gazed at Sami with such a wide, purple stare that Sami lowered her eyes.

"Natala is a rebalancer, like myself—a science and ritual specialist," Dorsom said, gesturing toward the young woman.

Sami touched her own chin. "You look—you look like—the caravan women—the Bedouin traders—from my teta's stories!"

"I'm not surprised," Natala said gently, then smiled. "You must be so confused right now."

"Try *totally freaking out*," Sami muttered. "I have no idea how I got here. Or even what *here* is."

Natala nodded. "Something . . . or someone . . . in Silverworld opened the portal and allowed you to enter. For now, we must avoid attracting attention, Sami," she said. "Try to keep your voice and thoughts lowered as best you can. Any crowd or great excitement will alert Nixie's soldiers."

"Nixie?" Sami frowned. "I feel like . . . I've heard that name . . . somewhere before."

Dorsom shook his head slightly as the waitress came out with a tray filled with small glasses. She placed sparkling lumps of something into the glasses, then lifted a Bedouin-style teapot with a curving spout high in the air, filling each glass with jets of tea. The air smelled like mint. "It's so good," the waitress confided, "to have rebalancers nearby. One feels much more secure."

The Flickers murmured and nodded politely and the woman bowed several times before she ducked back into the kitchen.

Natala shook her head. "Foolishness. Some Flickers believe locks can keep out the soldiers."

"We mustn't linger." Dorsom swirled a steaming glass. "Best for us to get back to headquarters."

"Please, though," Sami begged, turning to each of them. "Just—why do things look like home but not-home? How do I get back to my regular home? Where *am* I?"

Natala shook out a light veil and settled it over her head; tendrils of dark purple hair curled from the edges. "Sami, right now you're in a parallel World. You're an Actual being in a reflection-bound World—the other side of the mirror, you might say. Silverworld is shaped and changed by your thoughts, memories, imagination. And not just thoughts of your own life, but of the lives of your parents and grandparents, affect what you now see."

"And how do you even *know* so much—I mean, about me? My name and my grandmother and everything? I don't know anything about you guys!"

Dorsom laughed, resting one forearm on the table. His sleeve fell back so she could see a row of golden arrows tattooed above his wrist. "There is much to discover. But this is not the time."

The beautiful serving woman emerged again through a rustling curtain of beads, and placed large bowls of soup before Sami and Dorsom. Its smell was so rich and delicious, she felt almost light-headed. It was like inhaling soup from her earliest childhood—a scent of cumin and onion and lentils. She recalled her mother's contented hum as she bustled in front of a stove, Sami watching from the kitchen floor. Now she glanced back up at the waitress and Sami wondered if she'd been given soup that was on a menu or if she'd just tasted her own memory.

The server looked at her, startled. "Excuse me?"

Dorsom coughed loudly and asked, "Could you bring us more bread, please?" She nodded, but peeped at Sami twice over her shoulder.

As soon as she was gone, Dorsom whispered, "You must keep your thoughts lowered! In Silverworld, speaking through thoughts is as common as speaking out loud."

Natala shook her head. "She doesn't know how yet to control her abilities. And, Actual or Flicker, she's just a young girl—it's truly extraordinary that she's come this far without being detected!" She placed a hand on Sami's arm so her gray and black bangles jingled.

Sami bit her lip, surprised by her own emotions. This place seemed to magnify her feelings. Looking for a distraction, she picked up her soupspoon, enticed by the curling, warm aroma. The soup was a thick reddish brown and looked remarkably like her grandmother's *shorbet addis*—lentil soup. She blew on it and sipped from the spoon; it was hot and creamy. In fact, she realized, it was the most delightful thing she'd ever tasted. And then it was gone. Entirely. As if it evaporated the moment she swallowed. She blinked in surprise, then quickly took another sip. Again, there was the taste of cumin and onion and lentils, and then there was absolutely nothing in her mouth. "My soup! Where does it go?"

Surprised, Dorsom tasted a spoonful of his own soup. "What's wrong? It doesn't taste right to you?"

"It tastes wonderful. But there's nothing, like, *after* the taste! There's nothing to chew or swallow—just—air."

Natala's brows lifted. "Oh yes—you're missing the feeling of it."

"Ah, that's true," Dorsom said. "You Actuals are much more physical than Flickers. You rely on the sense of touch. Flickers—we are air and light beings. We don't actually eat or excrete in the ways that you do."

Sami stared at him. "You don't need to eat food? Why have cafés and, like, order stuff if you don't eat?"

The two Flickers laughed. "We do 'eat'—just not in the way you're used to," Dorsom said. "Our nutrients come through light itself. Photons instead of vitamins. For someone who was used to physical sensations, it wouldn't seem like much was happening when you ate in Silverworld. In this World, we're more concerned with what is seen than what is felt."

Sami finished the delicious and strange soup in about ten seconds. For a moment she was full, but then just as quickly the feeling dissolved. Before she had a chance to ask more questions, though, she sensed something like a current of cold pulse through the room. She looked around but all she saw was their waitress, smiling and asking if they'd like anything else. Sami was startled to feel the woman's pale eyes now pierce her like slivers of ice. Then, glancing over the woman's left shoulder, Sami noticed the very same waitress coming from the other side of the room. There were two of them. "Wait. What on earth?" Sami blurted.

The Flickers snapped to attention. Dorsom stood up. "Sami, get back," he ordered.

Sami felt another big throb pulse through the air.

This time it was deeper, a shock wave; it knocked the breath from her lungs. She seemed to be frozen in place as the waitress tossed her order pad, then began to grow, until the top of her head nearly touched the ceiling. Her features vanished and her entire body flattened into a shining white form. It was a deep swirling gray—just as if someone had cut out the shape of a person from the universe. The depth of the form was vast, and as Sami looked into it, it released a terrible, frozen shriek. With a gasp, Sami felt the thing reaching for her. Plates and cups were swept from the table as it wrapped her in its long talons. Shouting, kicking, arms flailing, she tried desperately to wrench herself free. The thing tightened its grip and seemed to press through her very body: Sami was falling into the emptiness and the emptiness was falling into her—a flattening void of sadness and surrender and loneliness.

She heard distant voices crying out, but the gray emptiness

only intensified. Without thinking, she steeled herself, then shoved, hard, against the thing. She struck with her mind, her will, her breath, her insides, tightening herself mentally, saying a great *NO* in her mind. There was a tremendous, swaying, tipping moment in which it seemed almost as if the thing would swallow her whole. Then she felt herself tearing free, icy strands ripping and shriveling and snapping.

Strong hands grabbed her arms, pulling her away. Stumbling backward, she saw the thing crumple and shrink. Then it oozed into a puddle on the floor and vanished.

9

Sami was weak and dizzy. Her legs felt squishy and her knees soft. She was having trouble catching her breath. "That thing—it grabbed me," she panted. "What *was* that?"

Dorsom slung an arm around her shoulders, steadying Sami. *You fought off a Shadow soldier! Never have I seen anyone do that before.*

Sami and Dorsom hurried out of the café, and Natala raced ahead, untied a couple of horses from a post in front, and beckoned. Sami shrank back warily. The horses were a deep goldenrod color that shone in the sun and their heads and necks were draped with engraved metal plates and rows of silver coins. They stamped their feet and snorted, their manes glittering. "Here—everyone, mount!"

"But—I can't get up there. I don't know anything about horses!" Sami cried. "I think I'm scared of horses."

Dorsom didn't appear to hear her, though, as he leapt onto a horse, then reached down, seized Sami's hands, and swung her up behind his saddle. Gasping, she clamped her arms around his waist and pressed her forehead to his back. Natala jumped onto the steed beside them. Dorsom snapped the reins and they took off.

At first she hung on with all her might. But bit by bit, her strength started to return and, instead of clutching Dorsom in terror, she began to relax. In time, Sami started to feel almost comfortable—as if she'd ridden on stallions before, even several times. Once she eased up, it seemed as if her body knew how to move with the animal, how to anticipate its bends and ripples. "Wow," she murmured as they flew along a wide lane of grass and sand. The wind rose, whirling in her hair. "Is this real?"

"What did you say?" Dorsom called.

Sami shook her head. "You still haven't explained what that thing was. Back in the coffeehouse? That came after me."

"Shadow soldier," Dorsom said grimly. "Straight from the Castle Shadow itself, judging by its power."

"They're shape-shifters. It did a perfect imitation of the server. And the way it absorbed you so completely—it was a creature of some rank." Natala looked over at Sami. *And it was stunning too that you fought it off.* Her thought emerged slowly and softly.

Gradually, the Flickers let the horses ease into a gentle canter. Sami turned to glance back at Dorsom. "That wasn't like any kind of shadow in *my* world."

He nodded. "I should think not. In Silverworld, the

Shadows are just as alive as the rest of us. For generations we coexisted in peace. These days . . . are different. Between us there's growing mistrust—it worsens all the time. There are normal Shadows—kind and generous. But then there are the soldiers and patrols of the Nixie's army. Which we must evade." He tapped the horse and they turned off the lane. They began cutting across a field scattered with bits of white stone and pieces of broken marble, like remnants of ancient statues. "Flickers are born of the color spectrum energy. Shadows are born of its absence. Between the two we cocreate our World. We need each other; we are virtually the same, only as seen from different directions."

"But then came the rise of the Shadow Nixie," Natala said. "Over the past several years, the rebalancers have measured a decreasing amount of color . . . and increasing Shadows." She gestured broadly. "There is terrible imbalance in Silverworld. Our crops are failing, the seas are deeper, more turbulent. Even the weather grows colder, the colors dimmer."

"Worst of all . . ." Dorsom's grip on the reins tightened as a soft breeze fluttered the horses' manes. "Flickers have started to disappear. Along with peaceable Shadows. More and more, across Silverworld. Our office is filled with missing Flicker reports."

"Nixie wishes to take over the Worlds. I believe she won't stop until Silverworld is plunged into eternal emptiness," Natala murmured.

Nixie. Sami turned the word over in her mind. Gradually, it came to her, the place where she'd heard that name before.

Nixie was a Shadow queen, Teta had told Sami, years ago. *Some say she was once a good and kind ruler. A being of the sparkling night reflection. And she fell in love with a magical creature, an* Ifrit.

Sami was four or six or eight, and her grandmother often told her stories about the reflecting world, the place where all the people in the mirror lived. Every actual person had their own private reflecting being. *Like a double,* she told her. Teta's was named Ashrafieh.

The Nixie was in love with her fairy Ifrit, Teta had said. *But eventually all the fairy species were starved or hunted to extinction. The Nixie went mad with grief. They say her grief changed her into a creature of rage. And she has remained this way ever since.*

Why is the Nixie angry? Sami had curled up on the carpet at her grandmother's feet.

A shadow had crossed Teta's face. *Sometimes, my child, grief does strange things. It can change the one who feels it. Sometimes it's easier to feel anger than sadness. The Nixie decided that if she couldn't have any joy, no one else would either. And from that day, she's made trouble, seizing joy and color and love wherever they exist—imprisoning any creature of happiness, both in the silver world—and in ours.*

Sami shivered at the old memory. She was about to ask Dorsom if her grandmother's stories were true, but they were distracted by a group of Flickers approaching from the opposite direction. The men, wearing long, shirtlike robes, were on foot, while women and children sat on rose-colored camels, one leg hooked before the hump, leather bags and goatskins dangling from the sides. Each of the women was of the same green color as Dorsom, their eyes and lips heavily tattooed, and strings of coins jingled in their black hair. As they approached, the green children gazed at Sami through their eyes bright with curiosity.

Road wanderers. Shield your mind, Sami, Dorsom thought.

He means, keep your eyes down, hide your thoughts, Natala instructed.

Sami tried to close herself off again, but she felt something like soft feathers tracing over her mind. As soon as the wanderers passed, she relaxed. *That's hard!*

You're doing beautifully, Natala assured her.

In this World, shielding the mind is a necessary skill, Dorsom added, *for self-protection and defense.*

Self-protection? Sami flashed on what had happened in the café and a shudder went through her. "What does the Nixie want with me?" she asked.

Dorsom and Natala exchanged a glance. "She's been watching you," Dorsom said. "She must believe you're useful to her in some way. When I realized you were about to Cross through the Silverskinned—the mirror—I suspected Nixie would send her patrol after you."

Yes, we know she has been studying you, Natala put in. *And so have we. We've been watching you for some time.*

Sami felt her neck prickle. "Me? Why?"

Dorsom patted his horse's neck gently, as if he needed more time for his answer. "We think you have a—a dual nature— part Flicker and part Actual. Your grandmother's family is well known in Silverworld—we've known about them for generations."

When you were born, the Silverworld sun brightened for some minutes, Natala thought.

Though that doesn't necessarily mean anything, Dorsom countered.

How could it not? Natala asked.

The two Flickers got wrapped up in a heated discussion that Sami couldn't quite follow and she turned away. Listening hazily to the beat of the horses' hooves in the fields, she wondered when the Flickers would tell her how to get home.

The soft light seemed to make her drowsy and stir up old memories. Hadn't her grandmother also mentioned the shadowy figures who came to steal babies? *They say the Nixie imprisons them, stealing their new energies in order to keep growing,* Teta had said. *Nixie was imprisoned in her castle and may only emerge once a generation, but her soldiers go out and snatch light creatures to serve in her army. And somewhere, deep in her castle, there exists a dreadful falling place, the rift between the Worlds. . . .* Sami recalled again the horrid, sucking creature who tried to seize her in the restaurant. She rubbed her arms, trying to press away her shivers. Then she remembered Teta always ended her stories by saying, *Someday, a brave warrior will come to them, someone with grit, and the courage of the* Ifrit.

Maybe all this time her grandmother had been trying to tell her something.

The horses moved more slowly, stepping over broken

plaster and stones. They were turning to the north. Ahead, Sami thought she could see a sliver of water and a strip of sand.

A smaller band of forest-green road wanderers appeared on the roadway. They'd almost gone by when a child stopped, staring, her eyes wide and brilliant. *Welcome, Silverwalker!* Sami felt the little girl's words ring through her.

The child's parents quickly reclaimed their daughter and hustled her back to the group, but her words remained in Sami's mind, puzzling her long after their group had gone.

10

The footpaths snaked through the fields, between mauve grasses and plum-tinted palmetto trees, and then, as the horses clomped up a low embankment, Sami was startled by the ocean waves coming into view. These weren't the usual Caribbean-blue currents of home. These ocean swells rose in the air in curtains of sea spume. They splashed and twisted slowly, more like veils than water. And the water was yellow. Sea yellow. Canary, daffodil, starlight yellow. The clearest color of sunshine. "Oh, just wow," she breathed.

"Beautiful, isn't she?" Natala said, then smiled. "She used to be even brighter—the Silverworld sea—not so long ago. Before Nixie."

Gazing out at the waves, Sami realized she really, *really* missed home.

Florida.

She'd never really considered its beauty before now. She hadn't appreciated it . . . until it was gone. Suddenly she felt she'd give anything for a glimpse of her mother or the sound of Teta's voice, and these things were wrapped up in the vanilla smell of the ylang-ylang tree and the bobbing ibis birds that grazed the neighborhood lawns.

"I want to go home," she mumbled, then looked hopefully at the Flickers. "Can I pretty soon?"

"You will," Dorsom promised. "I think."

"Soon, soon," Natala added. "Probably."

"*Probably?*" Sami cried. "You're not sure?"

"Almost sure," Dorsom said quickly. "We've never actually had a situation quite like this before."

"But pretty soon, I'm certain," Natala said. "No need to rush back, right?"

"I feel like—like I'm trying not to panic—but I can't even tell how long I've been here already. And my mom's going to freak when she realizes I'm not in my room."

"Your family won't have noticed your absence—not for a while yet," Natala said. "We move at accelerated speeds, compared to those of the Actual World."

"A Silverworld *week* fits into an Actual World hour." Dorsom straightened the reins. "Which is why people in the Actual World don't see us. When Actuals look into the Silverskinned, they see reflections, flashes, just blurs of brightness. Actuals only seem to see their own images, floating on *light*. But the light is *us*—the Flickers!"

"We've passed the morning." Natala pointed to the sun. "But in your World, hardly a minute's gone by."

They were trying to reassure her, Sami knew, or distract her, but somehow the thought of even *time* being different in this place made her feel even farther from home than ever.

The horses entered a small beachside village. It had sandy walkways, one blue cobblestone street down the center, and an assortment of squat buildings with shutters and window gardens washed in glimmering tints of amethyst. Dorsom and Natala hopped down and tied their horses in front of a lopsided little hut that looked familiar to Sami. It bore a small hand-painted sign over the door that said SILVERWORLD REBALANCING AND SECURITY.

"Thus far thus good," Natala said. "We've arrived!"

Dorsom helped Sami down; his expression was serious. "We may not be staying long."

"We're at . . . the pier. I think," Sami said slowly. "Back in my world, I mean. This is the old bait and tackle shop, isn't it? They sell frozen shrimp here. . . ." Sami smiled at the memory. Sometimes she and Tony got out their father's battered fishing poles, bought a bucket of bait and a few frozen candy bars, and dangled their feet off the pier.

"Not in Silverworld," Natala told her. "This is our office, and welcome."

Dorsom rattled a big bunch of iron keys. Abruptly, he stopped and said, "I smell fear." He squinted at the door a moment, then pushed it open with a squeak. *Shadow soldiers. You two wait here.* His thought was grim.

Standing behind Dorsom in the doorway, blinking, Sami could see wooden desks and filing cabinets with all their drawers yanked out, papers spilled everywhere. A big metal typewriter lay overturned on the floor. There was a toppled silver tray, an overturned Bedouin teapot, and smashed tea glasses. A ceiling fan with blades of woven palm fronds rotated lazily over the scene. Either the Flickers were horribly messy or their place had been ransacked.

They've gone. For the moment. Dorsom gestured for Sami and Natala to enter. There was a distinctive smell in the air—not unpleasant, but odd—a bit like the air just before a thunderstorm, heavy and briny and salty, as if the sea had just washed through the place. She touched a wooden cabinet that had been emptied of books. They were scattered in a heap, their splayed leather covers inscribed with symbols, much like her teta's spell book. She picked one up and ran her hand over its soft cover. *Somebody really doesn't like you guys,* she thought.

We're rebalancing agents. Natala's response startled Sami, who'd forgotten to watch her thoughts. Natala scooped up ledgers and papers from the floor and stacked them on the desk. "We have enemies."

"Apparently, the Nixie's creatures have just paid us a visit." Dorsom began plucking up a toppled pile of papers. "They don't usually bother with this much destruction. They're too busying recruiting Shadows and stealing Flickers and casting their cold length."

Their abilities are growing, Natala thought. *Deepening.*

"Their determination surely is," Dorsom added. "Truly they want you, Sami."

"*Me?*" She glanced over her shoulder. "But I don't have anything to do with this world—I don't even want to *be* here. What do they want from me?"

"Their queen is drawn to anything powerful—and threatening." Dorsom shook his head. "They might still be near. We need to take you to the Director."

Just then a low, resonating whistle filled the air and the Flickers froze in place. It was an eerie tone, more of a vibration than an actual sound. Sami felt the hairs on the back of her neck stand up. "What was *that?*"

II

The Flickers dropped their books and papers as Sami heard a powerful thought-voice, coming from someplace deeper than the bones of her head, booming out the words *I arise.*

"*That,*" Dorsom said, "is just exactly who we need."

Natala grabbed her hand and Dorsom unlocked a small door in the back that opened onto a little stoop, then wooden boards. The three left the shop and went out to the pier. It looked almost identical to the way it looked back in Sami's world, only these planks had a faintly violet hue. The boards extended far out over phosphorescent water, which looked semisolid close up, like a pudding or jelly. The end of the pier was crowded and streams of Flickers brushed past Sami's group, hurrying and chattering as if they were late to an important event. The men wore wrappings and scarves around their heads and necks and billowing floor-length jackets. The women were in floor-length garments that sparkled with red and purple embroidery. Some of the Flickers were deep green; others were hues of apricot and coral. Many had long, ropy hair, filled with braids, glass beads, and strings of coins. They held babies with smudged eyes, and talked and looked around anxiously, the men fingering strings of prayer beads—just a few of them seeming to note Sami with any curiosity.

"I think some of them know what I am," Sami murmured to Dorsom.

"It's more they sense what you're *not*," Dorsom whispered back. "Besides, they're too excited about the Director's appearance to pay attention." When Sami continued to scan the scene anxiously, he added, "Silverworld is more loving of newness and difference than is your Actual World. Here, Flickers enjoy it."

Sami also thought she detected several Shadows slithering among and through the Flickers. They seemed not quite three-dimensional—a bit like flattened misty-gray people. She felt chills run up her back and instinctively moved closer to her friends. "*They're* out here? Just on the loose?"

"These are not soldiers," Natala said quietly. "You must remember—Shadows are a natural phylum too. We coexist with them in peace . . . for the most part."

Dorsom checked the crowd. "It's the fringe group to watch—those that Nixie has claimed and trained for her purposes. We have a saying in Silverworld, Sami: 'The few don't stand for the whole.' There are many good and productive Shadows—there are even Shadow rebalancers."

Even after their reassurances, though, Sami still felt anxious and uncomfortable, knowing such creatures were so near and all around. She squinted, her eyes darting, but it was so dazzling by the water it was hard to see much. There were hardly any clouds in the sky and the palm trees on the beach wafted back and forth like they were trying to erase something. Sami silently worried and wondered about how she would ever get back home.

All at once, there was a commotion at the end of the pier. About two hundred Flickers began to shout and point and call out. And that's when she saw it.

The water sizzled and seethed, and a vast pink shadow moved like a wing under the water. The wind surged, forming whitecaps on the waves. Clouds filled the sky and the wind boiled, rocking the trees and grass. There was a deep roar and whipcrack, then a rumble that Sami felt all the way inside her bones.

Just as swiftly, the clouds rolled back and the howling wind died down. The water swirled, turned pink, and a gelatinous dome broke the surface. Sami watched the enormous thing rise: a translucent body, drifting tentacles, quills, hairlike spikes and fringes that swirled in the water and continued down into the depths. Inside its body a constellation of colors blinked and glowed with mysterious incandescence.

It floated in midair for a few seconds, big as a house, tentacles dangling in the water. Finally, sighing powerfully, the thing settled on the ocean surface, breaking the water into waves.

The Flickers began crying out and waving frantically, trying to get in front of each other. Sami heard "Rotifer" called over and over: *O, Greatness! O, Director!*

Sami felt a kind of hush fall over her in the presence of this thing, which was somehow powerfully ugly and beautiful at the same time. Its milky-clear tentacles swirled and sparkled and its body flashed. It didn't seem to have eyes or ears in its domed head, but she could make out a furious activity of shapes whirring through the pinkness, as if its thoughts took form as they came into being. "But—it's an *actual rotifer?*" Sami gawked. "We studied them in science—they're tiny. They're practically amoebas!"

"In *your* World," Natala gently chided.

"Rotifer is the oldest creature in Silverworld, born even before the realm of the Giants. It was there at the start," Dorsom said. "It founded the School of Rebalancers, orders of mystics and of alchemists, among many other guilds and societies."

"Between Flickers and Shadows, Rotifer is a species of in-betweens—part Flicker and part Shadow—shape-shifters, very powerful, called the *Ifrit*," Natala added. "Once a cycle, at sun-wane, the Director rises from its home waters to accept one question or request. For centuries, light beings have come to the pier to ask for guidance and favors." Natala's long hair lifted in the warm breeze.

"Just *one* question?" Sami's stomach fell in dismay. The pier was filled with Flickers. Hundreds more were arriving from every direction. All of them clamoring, calling to the great creature, many throwing roses, tulips, or lilies. The din was powerful—especially the thousands of thoughts, which Sami felt shouting, throbbing in her temples.

Natala slipped an arm around her waist. "Are you all right?" Her purple eyes glimmered with concern.

"This will never work." Sami gestured around in despair. "*One* question? I could come out here every day for a hundred years and never get to ask."

"In the past, it was much easier to gain an audience," Dorsom admitted. "Rare to find more than one Flicker waiting to consult with the Director. These days, they come in crowds, begging for help with their missing ones."

"But if ever we're getting you back to your people—this is it," Natala said. "Rotifer alone knows all the ways and paths between the Worlds."

Sami felt her chest tighten and her eyes grow hot. She stared at the masses of Flickers, squeezing in all around them. *Then it's hopeless*, she thought.

No, Dorsom thought back at her. She was barely able to perceive his thought against the background of Flicker thought-noise. *No*, he repeated. *Reach into yourself, for what you most want. You must have faith.*

It sounded just like something her teta would say. Sami took a breath, then frowned and mashed away her tears with the back of her hand. She trained her eyes on the great pink mass, half sitting in the water, half drifting. She released that breath and thought: *Oh, Rotifer, I just want to go home. Please, won't you please help me?*

Rotifer lifted a tentacle and pointed to someone else in the crowd. As the lucky one was chosen, a small cheer went up, as well as a number of sighs and protests. Then the Flickers nodded to each other, collected their things, and began to walk up the pier, back in the direction from which they'd come.

"Ah, already the Director has chosen," Natala said quietly.

Sami's shoulders sank in despair and Dorsom patted her softly on the back. She began to walk toward shore with the others. But before she'd even gotten halfway, Sami slowed down. She stopped. The crowd bumped and jostled around her, talking. The air was sparkling clear and bright and she shielded her eyes, trying to take it all in.

Sami started thinking. Wondering. Was there any possibility that she had come—or been brought—to Silverworld for an actual reason? It was all so weird and had happened so suddenly that it had felt like a mistake. But hadn't Teta's spell book opened to just that page and taken her right to just this place? Through all her shock and confusion, she'd never really considered this possibility.

She rubbed her arms, feeling a chill as the thought occurred to her: *What if I'm not supposed to go home yet?*

At just that moment, Sami sensed something happening—it felt like a gate opening within her body, a channel between herself and the amazing swirling creature. And a wisp of a voice had murmured, clearly audible beneath all the other thoughts: *Come here.*

12

Sami turned and began walking back, pressing through the crowd of departing Flickers, all of them now streaming off the pier, back to wherever they'd come from. She dodged and squeezed and ducked between Flickers, while several steps behind, her friends were calling to her and scurrying to catch up.

Heard you something? Dorsom asked. *In what register was the thought?* He scanned the last of the departing crowd as he took her arm.

The pier had almost emptied of Flickers and she could see that the great rosy Rotifer appeared to be addressing not a Flicker but a Shadow being. The Shadow's murky form was on its knees before Rotifer, its head bowed in silence.

Staring, Sami, Dorsom, and Natala came to a stop a short distance away. Sami tried to focus and pick up on their exchange of thoughts, but heard nothing—it had never seemed so silent inside her own mind before. The Rotifer lifted a tentacle and the Shadow remained motionless, but within the well of its body she saw what seemed to be pinpricks of stars glow and twinkle.

After this silent communication, the starry Shadow got to its feet and bowed low to the Rotifer. As it began to walk past the group of friends, it appeared to notice Sami. It stopped abruptly and Sami hesitated, afraid this was one of the creatures that were hunting her. Instead, it bowed deeply again and Dorsom and Natala bowed back. Finally, it straightened and went on its way, leaving her feeling unnerved, yet somehow honored.

One of ours, Dorsom beamed to her.

She watched, entranced, as the Shadow walked away. A moment later, she realized it felt as though her feet were buzzing. It felt, in fact, as if the buzz were climbing her legs, past her knees, and enveloping her body. It was a strange, lovely feeling, like standing in a cloud of stingerless bees—bumbling, light, soft bodies against her skin. She heard Dorsom calling, as if from a great distance, *Look!*

Lifting her eyes, she saw that the big tilting spikes had turned into wildly snaking forms, swirling in the air. She understood then that somehow it was reading or investigating her. It asked, *What Being are you?*

All at once it seemed as if somehow she'd gotten very light, as if there weren't enough weight on her feet. Sami was being lifted right into the air. The buzzing sensation now seemed to her like hundreds of fuzzy, vibrating balls of white light, fizzing along her body, carrying her easily, then placing her on the wooden planks directly in front of the gigantic Rotifer. She felt calm and happy, as if the white balls filled her with their soft opaque light. Even though the creature before her was three stories high and weirder than anything she'd ever seen, she didn't feel afraid.

The water around the great form shivered and the Rotifer swayed from side to side, its snaking spikes swirling wildly. Once again, Sami felt the low whistling sound that made her hair stand up. One by one, then, the balls of light dimmed and went out, and Sami sank closer to the pier. The two Flickers went to their knees, heads bowed. When the last bit of fuzzy light went out, her last bit of courage also seemed far away. She squinted up at the Rotifer.

"Intruder." Its voice tumbled, and the golden water surged and splashed high against the pier railing. "How come you into my World?"

Without lifting his eyes, Dorsom stood beside Sami. His hand on her shoulder wasn't enough to cut through the new fear she felt. She tried to speak, but for a moment her fear seemed to freeze the words inside her throat. "O, magnificent Director," he called. "It wasn't her fault! She didn't mean to Cross."

"Didn't *mean* to." The pink sides wobbled in the sunlight as its quills twirled. "How could some such creature—an Actual—puncture the SilverSkinned mirror and come to interfere with me and my creatures? Did the rebalancers somehow bring this about?"

"The mirror called to her." Natala also stood, head lowered, her hand on Sami's other shoulder. "It turned bright and liquid. Dorsom was alerted and he went to catch her."

"I had no way to warn her," Dorsom said. "I could only stand and watch her fall through."

"You are brave, rebalancers, to speak up for this outlander." Rotifer's quills slowed their frenetic activity and seemed to bend in Dorsom's direction. "It's your sacred mission to keep harmony and yet you defend an intruder. I could have you all swept away, broken into the cosmic dust!"

Sami felt its bellow rocking through her body and rattling her teeth. The air smelled powerfully of earth and rain, fish and mangroves. She was shaking, but she wouldn't let her friends take the blame. She stepped forward and blurted, "No! It's—it's not their fault. I'm the one to blame—the only one."

Silence, creature. The Rotifer blasted its thought, and she stumbled backward into the Flickers.

Then she felt something harden inside her bones. It was a bit like the old strength, the kind Teta had told her about. *The courage of the* Ifrit. She got back to her feet, though her knees wobbled, and she nearly lost her balance. She blasted a thought back: *I will not be silent.*

It had taken all her will to do it. She felt light-headed. But the big pink body dipped, light bending over its smooth surface. And if such a thing had emotions, she would have guessed it was feeling surprise. "Your nerve is impressive," the Rotifer finally said in its eerie low whistle of a voice. "Almost as great as your foolishness and arrogance. You have no business and no right being in this World." Now its long spikes pointed at her. They rolled with a slashing movement like the blade on her father's handsaw. "You are not worthless, it seems. Instead of dashing you out of existence, I think I shall incorporate you."

The pink creature tilted and moved its slashing head, revealing a wide-open jaw. The thought burst over her: *It's going to eat me.*

Dorsom bounded in between Sami and the Rotifer. *This must not be! I won't let you harm her.*

Then I shall be sorry to lose your valuable services, came the rumbling thought. *But there are other talented rebalancers who will try to fill in.* Its spike extended toward Dorsom, who stumbled backward into Sami.

Harm not this one, came a new thought. It was more wish than thought; it blurred and echoed and danced in weird, geometric prisms through Sami's mind. Through her glaze of fear, she saw that the Shadow creature had returned to the pier.

Rotifer reared upright. *You speak for her, Gray One?* it thought-roared.

I do, the Shadow hissed. *This one looked into me. I felt it happen. Sensation unlike any other. It saw fully.*

Sami realized that the "it" was her.

Is such possible? Rotifer demanded. *Did you gaze thus within the Shadow being?*

Sami's throat had turned papery with fear. She managed to think-hiss, *I looked at him—it—I guess. If that's what you mean. I didn't mean to*, she added hastily.

It saw me true, the Shadow said.

If such is so—the great body flexed—*what did you see?*

"Well, I saw just—a shadow—I mean, of a person," she stammered. "Like a paper cutout."

The Rotifer made a tootling snorting sound that might have been a laugh. "Any Flicker infant can describe the basic information of a Shadow!"

"And—and I saw it also had light," Sami added. She sensed the Flickers turning to look at her now. She concentrated, trying to remember the exact details. "It had stars. Inside of it."

For a moment there was no thought or movement. Even the spikes on Rotifer softened and stilled.

"They were like this." She dotted the air with her finger. "A bright blue star here. Three dimmer ones there, and there. A yellowish one over there. Lots of smaller ones sprinkled in the background."

The only sound was the sound of the water gently dashing up the pilings of the pier. Sami realized the Rotifer had started softly swaying or rocking—a movement filled with what seemed like a deep form of contentment, even pleasure. "So it truly is you. I had feared even to hope," it rumbled. "Samara Washington."

13

Sami felt a kind of mind hiccup at the sound of her name in the Rotifer's voice. Dorsom squeezed her arms without letting go and Natala moved closer.

"You described the constellation Cygnus, the Winged. Only *Ifrit* and Silverwalkers have the gift of DoubleSight. To gaze within both Worlds, to see the starry fields within Shadow beings, is a marvel beyond imagining."

The Shadow creature appeared to bow once again in her direction. "The honor was mine," it whispered. Then it turned and flattened into a sort of slot in the air. Sami heard breathlike laughter that continued to echo around them for a few seconds after the slot vanished into itself.

"Usually people only call me Samara when I'm in trouble," Sami muttered at last. "And I don't know what all this Silverwalker business is supposed to be about."

"You are one of them, the Silverwalkers—last of your kind," said the Rotifer. "Time ago, there were perhaps ten or twelve exploring the Worlds, but you are the first I've looked upon in two thousand years."

"But that can't be true!" Sami forgot about being scared and took two steps closer to Rotifer as the Flickers tried to pull her back. "I'm just a kid. I don't know anything about this stuff."

"*Enough,*" the Rotifer both thought and rumbled aloud. Sami felt the boards tremble under her feet, and her hands turned icy with fear. "If I truly had wanted to consume you, your parts would already be in my pharynx," it said. "There is no time. Not for examinations and confusions. You must learn your own nature on your journey."

Sami frowned. "My—what?"

Dorsom stepped forward again. "O, sublime Director, we came, in fact, to ask your assistance. We wish to Cross Sami back to her home. She Crossed to Silverworld accidentally—we want only to help her return."

"Accidental, 'twas not," the creature rumbled. "All Flickers know the Great Balance has shifted, that Nixie has thrown the Reflecting World out of true. Her crimes increase. This is beyond the power of gentle Flickers—even that of my rebalancers. This imbalance, I believe, is the reason why Samara was summoned into this World. *The Book of Silver* says: 'A double-being shall emerge, a child of Actual Nature and Flicker-lit, a child that shall Cross and See, a child named of soil and sand. That is the one who Stands Between and Restores.'"

"You don't mean *me?*" Sami felt something like tickly laughter rising up in her chest, the way it did in math class when she couldn't understand the problem. "I know Silverworld needs help, but if I get what you're saying—that I'm somehow this in-between Silverwalker person—well, I just don't think it's true. I'm *only* Actual! I don't have any of that Flicker stuff that you said. And you *have* to believe me. I can't save you guys! I can't even figure myself out."

Though she couldn't see its eyes, Sami had the strongest feeling that Rotifer was really looking at her, the way someone might study a book. The Silverworld sun had slanted in the sky and Sami noticed how its color had changed from a pale bluish light to a touch of bronze. There were Flicker birds roosting in the palm trees: back in Florida, they would be vivid green wild parrots, but here they glowed like handfuls of rubies, topazes, and emeralds and chattered in human voices, seeming almost to laugh and sing operatically.

"Samara," the Rotifer boomed at last. "I shall give you some words, then you must do what you will.

"Consider: freely you have walked the paths of Silverworld, undetected. Only my rebalancers—most sensitive and powerful of light beings—have perceived your true nature. Freely you read minds, you respond in kind. Yet, most above all, freely you saw into and detected the true nature of a Shadow being: that which shall not be seen. Such things no mere Actual is capable of."

"Nor Flicker, either," Dorsom added, glancing at Sami.

From the jaws of a Shadow Minion she pulled herself, Natala thought in a burst, adding out loud, "Extraordinary deeds she does perform, without understanding that she is extraordinary."

Sami sensed Natala was quoting from something, and she felt the same impatience as when Teta said that something was "written." *Written* meant that something—usually something bad, like her father's death—was supposed to happen, no matter what, and there wasn't anything you could do about it.

True Silverwalker, Samara Washington. The Rotifer broke into her thoughts. *The question is, do you accept your powers—and your fate?*

Sami waved her hands and shook her head. "I'm honored and everything. But . . . I—I just don't know." She turned to the Flickers. "I mean, reading minds is freaky enough. But that Nixie . . ." She shivered, thinking again of the waitress and the horrible sucking sensation. She turned back to the Rotifer, tightness in her chest. "I'm afraid if I try to help, I'll just disappoint you all—it'll just make everything worse."

"This only you can answer," Rotifer growled. The sky had turned a deep, bruised color and Rotifer's spikes and quills were once again whipping around. "The Shadow soldiers may already have scented you," it said. "They daren't attack while I'm here, but, choose you your home or journey, it's best you act before more of her Shadows assemble."

Again, shielding her eyes, Sami squinted at Rotifer, and realized the creature itself was turning the same eggplant color as the sky. Dark bands rose from its base as the water began to churn. A breeze picked up over the sky, blowing the hair back out of Sami's face as she looked over the horizon.

"Know this, Samara," Rotifer said, its voice growing hollow and echoing. "You are a Rejoiner: you must restore that which lies hidden. Without your help, all of Silverworld herself is in jeopardy."

The Flickers' thoughts rose up at this comment, churning in a wordless yet emotional agitation, but the Rotifer said, "Yes, and *soon*. On the gloaming, the Nixie will have her freedom. All light will be extinguished from Silverworld and the Shadow soldiers will have dominion over this dimension. And it won't end here, either. In your World, you will see your reflections lose light and sparkle. Eventually your World will also grow colder, the waters will cover the land, eventually your sun will begin to crackle and dim, animal and plant life will fade. Actual people will be swept from the planet. Nixie's dominion won't happen as quickly in the Actual World, but mistake not, it will begin. She will come."

At that, a tremendous wave cracked against the pier, throwing salt spray over Sami and the Flickers. *Accept you your journey?* The surf boiled with yellow waves. Sami looked into the swells and it seemed the waves were turning into wild beasts with foam fangs and glowing eyes. She moved away, drawn toward shore, wanting to be anywhere but where she was standing.

She took a few more steps backward, then turned, and found she was running as fast as she could, hands in fists, feet flying, away from the Rotifer and the storming water.

14

Sami blindly ran the length of the pier, hair whipping, eyes filled with tears, until she'd collapsed against the outside wall of the rebalancing office, curled up in a heap of misery. She'd landed in a scratchy, rainbow-striped bougainvillea bush and her feet sank into wet pink sand. Overhead, a flock of chattering birds settled into the trees, their calls sounding a lot like mocking laughter. Everything in this weird world seemed to be against her.

The Flickers caught up to her, panting.

We are here together. Natala pulled strands of hair away from Sami's face. *We will help you.*

Dorsom crouched beside her, his hand on her back. "Not a fear, Sami, please! We shall help. I promise you, truly."

Sami turned her face away. "How can you say that? No one

knows what to do! I'll never get home." Still, as they talked to her and patted her, she felt her emotions begin to shift, slowly altering, as if taking on different shades of colors. There was fear mingled with something like embarrassment mingled with wisps of hope. She wiped the tears from her face. Deep in the farthest corners of her mind, she heard a tiny whisper, her grandmother asking, *Is this how you were raised?* Gradually, she calmed and gathered herself. "Okay. All right." She straightened up, brushing at leaves and twigs, and taking a deep breath. "I'm all right, really. I just had to, like, throw a little fit, I guess. I'm better now." She realized Dorsom still had his hand on her shoulder and turned back in surprise. "Wait. Was that *you?* Did you just, like, *balance* me or something?"

Dorsom swiftly dropped his hands and clasped them behind himself. "Usually we'd have to fill out clearance forms. But time seemed to be of the essence, and so . . . ." His green face looked unusually pale with soft turquoise blotches.

She lowered her head thoughtfully, hands on her hips. "It's weird. Nothing's changed for me, except the way I feel. It's so much better like this. Rebalancing is *amazing*." She looked at Dorsom, wide-eyed. "Thank you."

Dorsom gave a modest nod. "Rebalancement is good for all beings—of light or shadow. For Actuals as well, it seems."

Dorsom and Natala suggested Sami spend the night with them in their headquarters—which was where the two Flickers both lived and worked. They could decide their next steps in the morning. Entering the building, Sami looked around nervously. Dorsom believed the Shadow soldiers wouldn't return right away, but Sami couldn't help scanning the room, waiting for the strange pulses of energy she'd felt when she'd first arrived. Her caution gave way to anger and indignation, though, as she once again viewed the ruined space. "This isn't right," she muttered, picking up notebooks and folders. "Those Shadow things—they shouldn't get away with this." She noticed a fat folder on top of the others in her arms, which said *Missing Flicker Reports*.

The three worked together, tidying the room, returning drawers and righting chairs, slowly restoring the place to order. Then Dorsom and Natala unrolled what looked like silky prayer rugs, much like the one Sami had found hidden in her room. They made her a bed of pillows and cushions so flat that Sami was sure she'd feel the floor underneath, but somehow the bedding buoyed her as comfortably as if she were floating in water. Dorsom stretched out on a thin mat on the floor beside her. *You don't have to do this*, she thought quietly to him. *You don't have to bunk beside me. You can go to your usual bed.*

This is where I sleep. Dorsom's thought reached her from his sleeping mat. *Besides, I'm already in dreams.*

She glanced back at his green profile. *Dorsom?* she thought-asked. He didn't seem to stir but she had the feeling he was listening. After a moment she thought, *There's something— I've been wondering. It's—I guess it's kind of personal, maybe. If you don't mind me asking . . .* His eyes remained closed, but she continued. *It's just—I've noticed a lot of, like, similarities—*

*between you and me. Kind of like in the way we think about stuff.
I don't know. Maybe I'm just imagining this, but my teta used to
say that people—I mean, Actuals—each have a reflecting angel,
like a Flicker of their own. My grandmother had Ashrafieh. And I
was thinking—I mean, I've been wondering . . . well, just, I have to
ask—are you my Flicker?*

Dorsom's eyes opened. He rolled on his side to face her. *You
have no idea how honored I feel.*

Honored? At once her face was burning hot. Had she said
something embarrassing? Or lame? She wasn't sure.

*Of course honored. That you feel we are so attuned and bal-
anced. Truly, I am—just, happy.* He grinned broadly. *Your teta
was correct—Flickers and Actuals are born in pairs, on either
side of the mirror. Flickers each have a sort of insight—an
understanding—of their Actual. The channels between us are ancient and secret, not well understood. Telepathic, I suppose, is the
Actual word. If an Actual is listening, open, paying attention to the
Silverskinned, Flickers can help them to know their deepest selves
and truest wishes.* He paused for a moment before looking back
up. *And, well, to your question, though—no. No, Sami. Much as
I wish it were true, truly I do, I am not your Flicker. But as a
rebalancer—*he lowered his eyes—*I am reflection to none.*

She nodded, trying to ignore a flutter of disappointment in
her throat. "Okay. Well, if that's how it works, I mean, then who
is my reflection?"

"Ah." His gaze lifted and again Sami had the sense that
she'd asked him something sensitive. "To the question of your

Flicker's identity . . . none of us knows the answer. We tried to find this Flicker when you arrived in our World. Natala looked it up in *The Book of Silver*. She found entries for all your family, yet no mention of you."

"How can that be? You said all Actuals have their own Flicker, right?"

He shook his head and rolled back onto the sleeping mat. "I don't know," Dorsom admitted. "It's unlike anything I've seen. Perhaps Silverwalkers are like rebalancers—born to be on their own. But perhaps someday I can help to Reflect you."

Sami lapsed into silence. She'd known almost nothing about Flickers before coming to Silverworld, yet now she felt oddly unsettled to think that no one knew who her Flicker was. She sighed and rolled over, certain she'd be up half the night, listening and waiting for the Shadows to come rippling through the air. But when she closed her eyes, she felt tiredness fall down over her like a thick blanket, and quickly fell into deep, dreamless sleep.

15

"Dumb birds," Sami muttered to herself. "Don't they ever stop talking?" She sat on the low tiled stoop behind the rebalancing office. Sighing, she gazed past the pier to watch swirls of magenta and cobalt in the sunrise curving up over the water. The Rotifer's words kept whispering at the back of her head: *Do you accept your powers—and your fate?*

The crimson birds turned in big circles, then swept low, close to Sami's head, the flock muttering furiously, seeming to echo and repeat the same debate in her head. *Accept you your journey?*

Dorsom emerged from the door and joined her on the back step. "Sleep well?" he asked. He set down a silver tray with two tiny glasses and poured steaming blue tea into each. There was a basket containing warm pita bread, a plate of fried white halloumi cheese, and a bowl of dried herbs. "We must not linger in this place, with the soldiers patrolling. However, a bit of breakfast will help us think."

Sami sniffed at the spice. "Za'atar! This is just like my mom does breakfast. She's an amazing cook, but she never thinks I eat enough."

Dorsom broke off some pita, dipped it in oil, and sprinkled za'atar on it. "This is still just thin Silverworld food, I'm afraid. But better than nothing."

Sami ate hungrily, once again disappointed by the way the food all evaporated when she tried to swallow it. But this time something else was attracting her attention. "Those birds." She gestured to the swooping, arguing flock. "Is that the usual way—I mean, in Silverworld—for birds to act?"

Dorsom peered in the direction Sami was pointing. The flock's deep scarlet hue seemed to streak in pink scrolls in the air. But Sami was talking about the way an odd stream of mist appeared to roll and coil between the birds. They squawked and flapped and pinwheeled, dipping and soaring and diving.

Dorsom stood slowly, eyes tracking the flock. "They are out of alignment. In distress, I think." He lifted his arms, walking out to the start of the pier, and closed his eyes. Sami felt a low rumble that seemed to emanate from his hands. The birds flew lower, then began to circle the Flicker, as if they were being pulled inward by a string.

Eventually they flew in a close red formation around Dorsom. He stood perfectly still, eyes closed, when suddenly he gave a sort of shudder. His hand shot out and the flock broke apart, flying off in a hundred directions. Sami thought they'd all scattered, but then she realized he was holding a bird.

It was plump and pigeon-shaped, and it seemed to be wearing a dark wrapper. Or trying to squeeze out of it. As Sami came closer, she saw the vapor move, swirling along its body, spiraling over its head, then wings, then tail feathers. The bird squawked and twisted as if it couldn't flap its wings.

Dorsom lifted the bird in both hands, filled his lungs, and began a kind of humming, which intensified until Sami felt it in her bones. Natala emerged from the headquarters and quietly joined them. No one spoke as Natala walked forward, her left hand lifted. She was wearing a large silver ring covering two fingers. Its gemstone flashed tones of deep purple and she nodded and said, "Three joules. It's near the deepest end of the scale. Fine to proceed." Then she looked around hastily as she stepped back beside Sami.

Now Dorsom lifted his head. The hum grew louder and more forceful, and the roiling shadow seemed to increase, covering more and more of the frantic animal's body, until Dorsom appeared to be holding a gray paper cutout of a bird. Then the shadow began to expand downward, covering his own hands and wrists. Sami didn't know what any of this meant, yet her breath sped up and her heart pounded. "Dorsom, be careful!" she cried out.

Suddenly, the bird gave a cawing, prehistoric shriek, and the shadow exploded into a spray of powder, vanishing into the air. Flapping wildly, the bird sailed off into the trees.

Dorsom's shoulders fell. For a moment, he stood, hands on his hips, head dropped, and panting for breath. Natala and Sami helped guide him to sit on the steps.

"Did you just—wow. What was that?" Sami sat beside Dorsom. "Did you just kill a Shadow?"

Rebalanced it. Dorsom shook his head. *Shadow escaped*, he thought breathlessly.

"Very powerful specimen," Natala said, gazing over the pier. "How did you manage to spot it? It's usually impossible to sight a midair Shadow soldier."

Still breathless, Dorsom pointed to Sami. Both Flickers turned to her.

"I didn't know what the heck that thing was," Sami protested. "Just that it looked pretty bad."

A bird fluttered down between Sami and the Flickers and cocked its head at her. "I owe you a debt."

Startled, Sami stepped back as the bird hopped toward her; it twitched its feathers and cocked its head in the other direction. Its sky-blue head tapered to a bib of white feathers down its front, its back glowed an unearthly bright red, and its feet were neon pink. *So—did that bird just talk to me?* Sami asked Dorsom.

In Silverworld, all living beings have language, he answered. His smile was still a bit weak.

The bird remained fixed on Sami. "I would have certainly died. No Flicker can see an airborne Shadow. Rotifer was right: you are a Silverwalker."

"You know about that?" Sami gaped.

"Our birds are marvelous eavesdroppers," Natala said with a smile. "And gossips."

Another bird settled beside the first in a flutter. This one had sea-green eyes. "She's ready, she is?" it said.

"Ready?" Sami looked from one to the other.

"For the back way," the first bird said. "Our gift to you."

"*Wait.*" Sami watched them carefully. "Do you mean . . . the way back home?" She felt a shiver of hope, despite herself.

"Call it as you will." A third pigeon, plumper than the other two, drifted down. This one had red plumage all over, but its beak glittered as if it had been cut from diamond. "We would like to—to thank you."

Ah, yes, Sami heard Natala thinking. *The birds—they would know.*

The plump one tipped its head. "In both Worlds we dwell, and regularly migrate between."

"Back, forth," the first bird said.

Sami was starting to understand. "Birds—live in both Worlds?"

"Hold on here," Dorsom cut in. "Sami hasn't had time to think about this yet—have you, Sami?"

The birds twitched their feathers. "No time for think. 'Tis leaving time now, if she wishes to go! She needs must make ready." The blue-headed bird lifted and lowered its powerful wings a few times. The breeze had grown steadily stronger and the sky was filled with high clouds.

"Wait." Natala held her hand out. "We must consider."

Sami rubbed her arms—they were all gooseflesh. These birds were offering to help her get home! Yet for a moment she held back, thinking of her grandmother, wondering what Teta would have wanted her to do. Was she meant to be here, as Rotifer had said? But it was so hard to think of staying when suddenly there was a possibility of going home.

"If we are to do this," the red-gray bird said, "it must be now." The birds hopped out to an open stretch of grassy, sandy land that rolled along the beach. There were no palm trees, just rich, jade-colored blades of beach grass that glowed brighter as the sky darkened.

Sami walked toward them, shaking her head. "I'm grateful, really, this is so kind—but I'm not sure . . ."

Sami noticed then that several more birds had arrived. In fact, more and more were fluttering down to crowd around her feet, the three original birds piping and twittering in what sounded just like birdsong from the Actual World, bright and sprightly.

Very quickly then, dozens, hundreds of birds were landing, crowding the grass, milling around, jerking their heads, moving stiff-legged, chirping, and hopping. Many were pigeons, but there were also spotted pink parrots, and ibis that glowed like opals, and herons that looked like they'd been dipped in liquid gold. There were canaries, macaws and sparrows, seagulls and pelicans, and one that lifted its tail into a snow-white peacock fan.

"Prepare yourself!" the red bird called out.

"Wait—guys—I need to tell you—I'm really not sure about it," she said cautiously.

"It's time, it's time!" a coral-colored falcon screeched.

"But wait—I—I think maybe this isn't the right time after all," Sami blurted. "I can't do it. Not right now." But the birds were making a racket of flapping and chirping, none of them listening. She could see Dorsom and Natala getting crowded out behind a wall of beating wings.

"We shall begin!" one of the pigeons cried. The birds started hopping up her legs and fluttering on her arms and shoulders. Sami gave a tiny yelp and a parakeet on her head jumped off, but they kept coming, batting their wings in her ears and face, and it was all she could do not to beat them away.

"Stop, wait!" she shouted, pulling in her arms. But they just kept climbing and batting. Another bird voice shrieked, "*Lift, lift, lift!*" All at once, the toes of her sneakers were sweeping the ground, her T-shirt and jeans yanked up high, a hurricane of feathers and bird voices and bird cries. In another moment, she was looking down and the two Flickers were below, jumping and shouting. *Birds—return her at once!* Dorsom thought-called.

Instead, they kept rising, the birds climbing on the wind. "Put me down!" she yelled, but none of them could hear her in the thunder of flapping. They were quickly very high. Below them the wind was tossing around the palm trees, their big fronds slapping and waving. The birds struggled a bit, jostled by the gusts. Her hair slapped at her face and she couldn't brush it away as every bit of her was pinned by birds. She craned, and twisted her head, and glanced up to the clouds.

There was an odd shift in the light, a sort of sparkling overhead. Sami blinked through her hair and the dazzling light, looked directly into the sky, and saw her grandmother's face.

16

Teta's face was right there, inside a clear section of sky, looking to Sami like someone had placed a movie screen directly over her head.

Teta!

It occurred to Sami that she might be seeing through some sort of portal or mirror in the sky. Her grandmother's gentle eyes gazed through the clouds, and Sami wanted to call out to her. She felt almost sick with longing, but seeing Teta's sorrowful eyes reminded Sami of what was at stake. This was why she'd come to Silverworld in the first place. It became clear to her: it wasn't time to return, not yet. She still didn't know how she would accomplish it, but she'd come to save her grandmother, and that was what she would do.

The wind was blowing even harder now and her skin stung

from the colder air. Sami felt prickly all over, scared and alive. Her hair slapped her eyes, and for several moments almost all she could see or hear was the hurricane of flapping wings. Teta's face grew larger and blurrier as they approached the portal. Then Sami thought she noticed something flash behind Teta's face. It happened again, a sharp, dark form.

A castle?

It had flashed just twice, but Sami sensed she hadn't been meant to see it at all—it was a bit like catching a glimpse of the tricks behind a magic show or the hand inside a puppet. What had she seen? She tried narrowing her eyes, then discovered that if she closed her eyes completely she could pick up on images from the minds of the birds—they were all focused on a destination—the place they were actually taking her? Gradually, Sami made out a shimmering castle, snapping flags, rolling lawns and topiaries, then, superimposed over all this, there was the image of a single eye, wide open. It was the same clear blue color as the sky in the Actual World.

Suddenly, she felt a dip, as if several of the birds had flinched at the same time. *What? What?* She heard question-thoughts popping through the flock.

There was a gray blur at the corner of her eye and a thought blinked into her head, saying, *Silverwalker, you are reading us. This is not allowed.*

This isn't the way back at all, is it? she demanded. *Where are you taking me?*

Sami's body started twisting in the air, one leg lifting, an arm bending back, as the birds became jumbled and chaotic thoughts bubbled through the flock.

Do not make this difficult, the red bird thought-croaked. *We are under orders.*

Sami was swept around in the rush of wings and wind and hair and clothes. Hundreds of claws pinched through her shirt and cut into her skin, but her resistance only grew stronger. As the birds continued to ascend, Sami summoned as much will and focus as she could and thought: *Let go of me.*

Something happened in the red bird's thoughts that felt like a mental shudder or twitch. Instantly, something rippled through the flapping, squawking flock, a snaking current, and all at once the entire flock of birds turned murky.

Like shadows of birds.

You're Shadows! Sami yanked and thrashed her arms desperately and broke away from a few of the claws. Now she knew that—wherever they were trying to take her—it was definitely a place she didn't want to go.

Inches from the clouds, Sami reached out as she felt herself slipping. Teta's face was too close to see, blurring into shapes and colors among the clouds. Sami's hands swung out as she spun, brushing through creamy softness, and grazing something that felt almost like skin.

Grab her! Catch the Silverwalker! the birds thought.

She was falling. Everything turned white and wet; frozen

droplets scraped her arms. It was like falling through clouds—only the clouds were supposed to be over her head, not under. Cold zinged through her body, her lips and lashes frosted over, her skin turned to ice, the World turning into a Milky Way swirl.

17

And then.

She was sitting unharmed on the red Persian carpet on the floor of her bedroom. Blinking, astonished, Sami breathed in familiar scents of wool, trees, and lavender, and slowly came to understand that she had fallen back into the Actual World. There was not a scratch on her. Her hair and clothes felt a little damp, but aside from that, there was no sign of her struggle with the birds or Shadows or anything that had just happened.

Lifting her eyes, she glimpsed her mirror bobbing and glowing silver before it whitened and hardened back into glass.

She'd *done* it; Sami could hardly believe it. She'd pushed against the Shadow birds and tumbled through the portal. Sami had no idea how she'd managed it, but she was beginning to wonder if she could possibly be a Silverwalker.

She had to tell Teta!

Sami ran down the hall to her grandmother's room. "Teta, you will not *believe* this. I did it. I went into the other world! And they need my help—they need—"

"Shhh!" Her mother looked up, dark curls tumbling around her neck. She was crouched beside Teta's bed, a steaming teacup in one hand. "Sami, lower your voice!"

"Mom!" Sami skidded to a stop.

Alia placed the teacup on the nightstand. Teta was tucked into bed, even though it was the middle of the day. "Please quiet down—your grandmother is very tired. We just got out of the doctor's office and she started running a fever on the drive home." She bent back over the older woman. Teta looked small and pale in her bed, as if she'd somehow shrunk while Sami was gone. Her eyes were shut tight and she seemed to already be asleep.

Touching Teta's forehead, Alia waited a moment, then straightened. "Samara—are you all right? What're you up to?"

Sami lowered her eyes. She couldn't let her mother see what was bursting inside her. There was no time for that. Once Alia's suspicions were raised, she wouldn't let it go—there would be questions from now till next year. "Mom. It's nothing. It's just a—a game Teta and I are playing. A make-believe thing."

Alia fingered the necklace at her collarbone. A gift from Teta, the little silver charm was called a hand of Fatima, meant to ward off the evil eye. "Oh really?" she asked drily. "A game?"

Her mother was getting her skeptical attorney look. Sami

had to think fast. Her eyes swept around the room and landed on the row of aromatic spices Teta kept in tiny glass jars on her dresser—turmeric, cumin, and za'atar—which were supposed to restore health and clear the mind. Then she had a brainstorm. "Mom, I am so hungry," she said, which was true. "I'm totally, totally starving. In fact, I'm dying for some of your kibbee. Can't you make some, pretty please?"

Alia drew in her chin, then started laughing. "I can't keep up with you—one second you're shouting and running and the next—" She broke off, studying Sami in bemusement. "You really want kibbee?"

"Actually, can you make, like, a couple of those old dishes? Like you and Teta used to make together?"

Alia stared at her daughter. "You mean—something Lebanese?" Her smile was tentative, but Sami could see she'd managed to surprise—and distract—her mother. "It's been a while," Alia said. "I guess I could come up with a few things. Oh, come on—let your grandmother rest. Let's see what we've got in the fridge."

Downstairs, Sami joined her mother in the kitchen. The two of them began pulling ingredients from the back of the cupboard—bulgur and beans—and rummaging in the refrigerator. The dishes she'd asked for—kibbee with minced lamb and onion, tabbouleh salad with parsley, and okra in spicy tomato sauce—took a lot of preparation and work, which would keep her mother preoccupied. While Alia stirred and combined, Sami cleaned and chopped, her hands moving swiftly and effortlessly, as if she'd done this all her life. At the same time, her mind was far away in Silverworld. Noticing Sami's swift knife work, including a series of radishes she carved into roses, Alia asked, startled, "Where did you learn to do that?"

"I don't know!" Sami admitted with a laugh.

Her mind and senses felt supercharged, brighter, as if she were processing things in a new way—her mother's long hands, the crispy meat in the kibbee, the recording of Fayrouz that Alia had put on in the background, the palm trees swaying in the kitchen window. She saw, felt, and tasted every detail. Setting out plates, Sami went over and over the meaning of the images she'd seen in the sky: the castle and that deep blue eye. She listened to the elegant singer, her voice swooping and rising in Arabic, and she realized she could understand about half of the words—this was also something new. She'd grown up listening to her mother and grandmother converse in Arabic—it was a private language, just between the two of them. Alia wanted Sami to speak English. Sami never imagined that she had learned any of it, even accidentally.

But there wasn't time to puzzle over this. She ate quickly, nodding at her mother, but in reality she was barely listening as her mother fretted about the doctor's advice and Aunt Ivory's opinions. Then Alia said, "I guess Ivory is right. It really is time to get your grandmother into assisted living."

Sami came to attention. "What? No. That is, like, the *last* thing Teta needs right now. She needs to be with us, with her family."

"Sami, I understand you're upset—"

"I'm not upset—I'm *right*!" Sami sputtered. It was true—

she was getting upset, but she couldn't seem to help herself. "*Dad* would *never* have put Teta in a home. Why do you even listen to Ivory? She's so mean!"

"Samara Washington." Her mother put down her knife and fork. "How dare you say such a disrespectful thing about a member of your own family? What in the world has gotten into you?"

"Why should I respect her when she doesn't respect me or Teta?" Sami put down her own fork and sat back. She couldn't believe she was speaking to her mother so directly but she couldn't seem to hold herself back. "Why should I respect someone who doesn't deserve any respect?"

Alia turned bright red. "That is quite enough, young lady. Get to your room right this instant!"

18

Sami marched up the stairs indignantly. Then she waited behind her closed door, and as soon as she thought her mother wasn't watching, she crept down the hall to the room on the left.

Tapping softly on Teta's closed door, Sami opened it a crack. It was dim in the room, as usual; the daylight filtered through the half-cracked shutters. Her grandmother was lying in bed, but her eyes opened as Sami entered. Over her shoulder, her reading lamp illuminated the silhouette of a row of tiny camels. Teta's room had a lovely smell of sunlight on sand—a memento, Teta claimed, of years of crossing the desert floor as a Bedouin tribeswoman. Coming closer, Sami was startled by how small her grandmother appeared to be. Her silver necklace looked bigger on her chest and her ring was loose on her finger. Sami crouched by the older woman's side and took her hand. "Teta? Are you okay? How do you feel?"

Teta pressed her lips together, moving one hand to wave off Sami's concerns.

Sami frowned, but she knew there was no use asking questions when her grandmother was like this. "I have to tell you—ugh—I've got *so* much to tell you!" Unsure of where to begin, she hesitated. Teta had always told tales of other worlds and magical beings, but what Sami had to say felt different: bigger, realer. "The thing is, I found your book of spells. . . . The one you'd hidden under my bed?" she began. Her grandmother nodded slowly. "I was looking for, like, a treatment. For you—I mean, the trouble you have—with talking?"

Her grandmother shook her head.

"Well, yeah, then I opened it up." She stood, stepping back from the bed. Teta placed one hand on the base of her throat. "I know—I know! I'm not supposed to open it till I'm twelve. But I *had* to. There's stuff going on with Mom and Ivory. Just, trust me—I had to. The book led me to the right page and I read it and—"

Sami broke off—was that her mother coming up the steps? Not yet. She swiveled back and whispered, "*The mirror opened, Teta! It opened* right up and pulled me in, and—and—Wait . . . wait." She studied her grandmother's face for a moment. "Why aren't you saying anything?"

Teta lowered her eyes and studied her fingernails. Finally, she looked up at Sami and said, "Ennnh laa basha?"

Sami shook her head. "No, Teta, it's me, remember? You talk normally to me."

Teta opened out her hands in a kind of hopeless gesture. "Boookh aadoo!"

Sami's entire body felt cold and there was a dizzy pressure between her eyes. This was bad. This was very, very bad. Sami was the only one left who could understand Teta—without their link, there would be no hope of saving her from Ivory's horrible plan. Instead of panicking, though, she nodded and took a deep breath. "Okay. Okay. This is all gonna be fine. I think. But I need to ask you a question. The thing is—when I was there? In that other world? I saw something, like in a dream. I saw a castle, and a—a big blue eye."

Teta's own eyes widened.

"It sounds weird, I know. But I guess it wasn't so much a dream, it was more like a—vision, I guess." She dropped her voice nervously as she said this, though she knew that her grandmother believed more in visions than she did in the evening news. "I've got to get straight back to Silverworld, but first I need you to tell me what those things are. The castle and the eye? Are they real? Are they places?"

Teta shook her head, but Sami couldn't tell if she was saying no or just saying that she didn't know. Or that there was no way for her to explain it.

"Teta, please—this is super important. Isn't there *anything* you can tell me?" she begged.

"SAMARA SERAFINA WASHINGTON." Her mother was standing in the doorway, hands on her hips, her face like a thundercloud. "I thought I told you to go to your room."

Sami dropped her head, deflated. "Sorry, Teta. I gotta go." As Sami bent to embrace Teta, her grandmother secretly pressed something into Sami's palm. It felt hard and cool in her hand, and Sami thought she felt a silvery current race up her arm. Something like tiny bells softly tinkled in her ears. Teta turned and gave Sami a single grave nod.

19

Back in her own bedroom, Sami closed her door firmly, pressed her back against it, and opened her hand. Her grandmother's sapphire ring glittered in the middle of her palm. She inhaled sharply. Her grandmother never took her ring off. She marveled over it—why had Teta given this to her? Was it just another sign she was sliding into dementia? Sami thought of the many childhood afternoons she had spent gazing at the ring on Teta's small hand and admiring the deep blue currents that seemed to wash through that stone. Teta claimed it had been given to their family centuries ago by a genie. Other times she said a mermaid. It was supposed to carry a spell of protection that would defend anyone who wore it. Yet when Sami slid it on, it slid right off again, too big for her finger.

At the moment, though, she had a more pressing problem

than figuring out the ring: Sami couldn't find the spell book. She needed its instructions on how to get back to Silverworld. Had Teta taken it? Had it fallen through the mirror when she first entered? She rummaged through her bedroom, hunting under blankets and furniture and pillows, begging, calling to it under her breath: *Where are you? Where did you even go?*

Slowly, the reality of her situation became clear: she was going to have to get back to the other World on her own.

She took a deep breath, stood tall, and studied her whole mirrored reflection. *I can do this.* She did feel different—straighter, more herself. She had a clearer, truer sense of things, which seemed to have traveled back with her from Silverworld. This wasn't a game any longer—Teta really was failing, and Sami would have to act quickly. Time to get serious. *Flicker? Whoever you are . . . if you're even there . . . I need you now.* She tried to send her hope, gratitude, and desperation through the glass. If Dorsom was right, she thought perhaps her own Flicker had been the one who first helped her pass through the mirror into Silverworld—and would, she prayed, help her do so once again.

"I need to get back," Sami whispered to the mirror. She tapped lightly on the cool surface with the sapphire ring. "Knock, knock, let me in! I thought this ring was supposed to be magic," she said, indignant. Letting her fingertips trace the glass surface, she tried to remember what Teta had told her about communicating with the reflecting beings: dreams, prayers, visions, spells, rituals. . . . The sorts of things that were all described inside the missing spell book.

"I was supposed to be a Silverwalker!" she cried in frustration. She remembered her mother saying the only way out was through. "How can I go *through* if the door won't open?" Her arms fell against her sides and she felt something rustle in the pocket of her jeans. She reached in, then drew out a sheet of golden paper folded into the shape of a star. It was beautiful and featherlight and she'd never laid eyes on it before in her life.

She turned the paper over and over: it was clearly some sort of magical token. She held it up before the mirror. "Is *this* what you're looking for?" The mirror remained still and silent.

Perhaps something was written on it? Carefully, with trembling fingers, she unfolded the bright paper. With the last delicate fold, a stream of brilliant blue powder spilled through the air, a sky-blue plume glistening in the air before the mirror. On an impulse, Sami reached out, waved her hands through the plume, and the jeweled blue dust clung to her skin like sleeves, tingling up and down her arms. This was clearly some kind of magic—but was it the right kind? "All right." She turned back to the silver surface of the mirror and lifted her arms. "What do you say? Let me in!"

Her eyes widened as the center of the mirror began to glow. Quickly, a half-familiar feeling stole over her—that sensation of her center of gravity shifting. She leaned closer to the mirror, the way a person might peer over a diving board. After one more breath, Sami closed her eyes, put out her hands, and let herself keep going. She fell forward toward the mirror, swiftly at first, with a gasp, and then it felt as if the air thickened and she was passing, gently, through the silky Silverskinned, the sparkling blue sleeves parting the glass, then peeling away from her arms. And it seemed in that instant that she had dreamed of that very same sensation many times in the past.

Once again, she was tumbling.

Clouds hurtled toward her in a blur of turquoise and lavender and birds spun away chattering and treetops appeared, and all she had time to think was, *Too fast!*

20

Sami woke with her arms out, her head rocking back and forth. She was lying down, covered with a loose, soft blanket. She moaned and squinted, looking around, but wherever she was was dim, with a few slivers of light that hurt to look at directly. She closed her eyes: the place smelled powerfully of bark and dirt—a good smell, in fact, and she relaxed into it. The scent reminded her of her old neighborhood in Central New York, the fields across the street where she went looking for frogs, and tiny crickets sprang through the air like musical notes, and she collected pussy willows and cattails and brought them home in a bouquet for her mom. Back when her mom still smiled a lot, and she'd bend over Sami, touching her head and saying . . .

"You awaken, Sami! Oh, thank Rotifer!"

Sami looked up: it was Natala, bending down, her purple

eyes filled with concern, her hand brushing over Sami's forehead. "What a fall you had! It was extraordinary-spectacular."

Sami eased onto her elbows slowly, blinking. She felt achy and bruised, but nothing seemed to be broken. "I hardly remember—"

She could just make out Natala's subtle smile in the shadowlight. "We saw you struggling, those birds taking you up, up, then all of a sudden flying off you, one by one. You fell upward, straight skyward, into the portal. It was quite something. We've watched the skies ever since you Crossed back, hoping for your return. Fortunately, when you fell back to us, you didn't have near the weight here that you did in the Actual World."

Now Sami sat up and stretched out, then bent her legs and her arms, groaning and surprised that she was still in one piece. "I remember . . . those birds—I think they were Shadows! I fought them off and landed back in the Actual World. But the birds were trying to take me somewhere else—I can't remember exactly." Sami shivered and hugged her knees.

"We were afraid of such." Natala nodded grimly. "Shadows are shape-shifters—they take on the form that serves them. And Shadow soldiers will shift to hide their dark purposes."

"Where are we now? What is this place?" Sami reached out to one side and touched an arching, braided surface. It felt like the inside of a large basket, about six feet high, and not much wider across.

Natala looked around, her face wary. "This is a ground hut."

"A ground what?"

"A sort of abandoned warren. The Shadows, they used to dig them out and use them to nap and get away from the light." Natala swiped a ringlet of purple hair behind one ear. "More and more, the Shadows must hide from Nixie or be imprisoned by her. All their old relaxing places, like these ground huts, or the wells, or the caves—the places they once liked to gather— have been mostly emptied. These days, there are far, far fewer good Shadows about than there ever used to be. Now they are soldiers. Or they are prisoners."

Sami leaned back again on her elbows. Her body ached and her head felt heavy. "So Nixie steals her own creatures? There's got to be some way we can help those Shadows."

"No light being—Shadow nor Flicker—has ever been reclaimed from Nixie, I'm afraid. No one dares make the journey to the Bare Isles." Natala smoothed her hand over Sami's forehead. "Oh, once Silverworld was filled with marvels—fairies and fauns, flying horses and griffins—all manner of betweencreatures, *Ifrit*, which are part Flicker, part Shadow. But no more. All stolen by the Nixie."

There was such a gentle, familiar lilt to Natala's voice that Sami couldn't help giving in to its music. Sinking back sleepily, she noticed streaks of hazel in the Flicker's dark purple eyes. "Are you my mother's Flicker?" she asked, half drowsing as the Flicker stroked her head.

Natala laughed softly. "Oh no, my dear. I'm like Dorsom—a rebalancer. When Rotifer selects the child-Flickers who will become rebalancers, we sacrifice our lives of reflection." She looked thoughtful for a moment. "It can be a rather lonely life for a Flicker. Light beings take much joy and satisfaction from the relationship with their Actual."

Sami could feel the emotion in Natala's eyes as if it were a real weight pressing down on her chest. She thought again of her mother, her wistful expression when she talked about Lebanon.

Natala's eyes sparkled. "Don't fret, Sami! It's amazing, a great honor, to be a rebalancer. Never would I trade."

Something scuffled over their heads and both Sami and Natala froze. A bolt of light opened at the top of the hut, and Dorsom jumped in, pulling the hatch shut behind him.

Dorsom crouched beside her, a large canvas sack slung over his shoulder. "Sami! You are whole! Those birds—"

"Shadows. She knows," Natala said.

"I snuck into our headquarters for supplies," Dorsom said. "But we shouldn't go back there anymore. The whole place is Shadow-swamped—they're watching every door and window. This is a safe place for Sami until we can decide on our next move."

Sami shook her head. "I saw something—when I was up—above—with the Shadow birds? I saw things right in the clouds! First I saw my teta's face. It was like watching a movie in the sky. . . ."

"You saw through the portal!" Dorsom exclaimed.

"But there was more. I kept getting, like . . . flashes of something—like pictures hidden behind my grandmother's face. I saw something—a gray castle, I think. And a weird blue eye." She shivered.

"The eye is mysterious-strange." Dorsom shook his head. "And there's only one remaining castle I know of in all Silverworld."

"That of the Nixie, the Castle Shadow," Natala agreed.

"Also, Teta gave this ring to me—right before I came back." She pulled it out of her pocket. Both Flickers bent over her fingers. "She snuck it to me, but I don't know why."

"Very lovely indeed," Natala said, studying it closely.

"An old stone," Dorsom observed. "Possibly a powerful one."

Sami rubbed the gem's facets. It seemed to whisper to her; she felt odd longings and emotions rising from its surface. And yet she knew this was all in her imagination. She'd hoped the ring would somehow show her more or explain something, perhaps release more of that blue magical powder, but mostly it just looked pretty. She tucked it back into her pocket with a shrug. "I think—I think . . . maybe I have to go to that Castle Shadow and confront this Nixie," she said to the Flickers. "If I'm ever going to help my grandmother—I have this idea—it's something to do with the Nixie."

"Oh no! No, no." Natala shook her head. "That would be a disaster. She would capture you—or worse. . . ."

"Nixie has what the Actual needs." This comment came from a new voice—soft yet piercing, like a scratch on the air. Sami peered through the gloom until she saw the outline of a small pointed snout and a pair of wings, hovering near her feet.

"I saw what you did—with the bird flock," the tiny shriek continued. "'Twas lovely to me. And surprising—which I like."

Sami kept searching the thatched hut. "Who are you?"

"Shadow bats," Dorsom murmured.

Natala scanned the darkness. "I thought they'd all retreated to lower caves."

"Bats are the eyes and ears of Silverworld." Dorsom turned to the small animal. "Please tell us—what do you know of the Nixie and her castle?"

Sami had a weird feeling that the Shadow bat was smiling. Its scratching voice said, "Not for you will I say, but for her."

She flinched as a whisper of wings fluttered past her hair and seemed to alight somewhere behind her right ear. "You are a Silverwalker, Samara, Rejoining and Righting One," it creaked. "There is tale upon tale of Nixie's powers and ways. And prisoners. Many, many Night Creatures have been taken. And Flickers, too. One in particular—a powerful, old Flicker. When it comes time of the gloaming, when the strength of night is at its fullest, Nixie will be at the height of her power. She will range and hunt and absorb magic, as she absorbs all within her territory."

We'll go nowhere near the Castle Shadow. Natala shuddered. Especially *at gloaming.*

"Nixie knows the Silverwalker is here," whispered the scraping voice. "She plans to lure Samara into her kingdom. She means to trap and imprison her—just as she brought her here, through the Silverskinned."

Treachery, Natala thought.

We won't be lured by Nixie or her Shadow tricks, Dorsom added.

The Shadow bat snapped its wings. "Listen to me, Flickers! The Shadow realm is your only hope if you dream of vanquishing the Dark One."

Dorsom started to object, but Sami broke in. "No, I think the little bat is right," she said. "If I want to help my grandmother—and you want to save your world—we've got to go after the Nixie."

After a long moment, Dorsom nodded. "I agree. If we are to do it, we needs must work with Shadow beings—they know Nixie's ways far better than any Flicker does."

"Flickers never like to look in Shadow corners, in cracks and under rocks, but that is how you will find your way," the bat voice scraped. "You must travel and cross the Darkling Straits, enter the Bare Isles, and make the journey to Castle Shadow."

Natala began to protest. *That's impossible. It isn't safe. If we're anywhere close to the Bare Isles, Nixie will surely discover us.*

The Shadow bat's laughter sounded like pebbles raking over pebbles. "Foolish one—Shadows can spot Flicker light from great distances. You Flickers strut around and never think about what the Shadows observe. There *is* no 'safe' if Nixie is hunting for you."

Sami's eyes had adjusted enough to the gloom that she could make out Dorsom's face, lost in thought, while Natala stared at the ground—both of them silent and brooding.

"Stay or go—to me, it makes no difference whether you let the Bleak Fairy capture you or dash you into the cosmos," the Shadow bat said. "I care about Samara and Silverworld. If she wishes to do it, I will help her make this journey."

Sami realized then that the Flickers had stopped listening. Natala's dark purple head was lifted; Natala was tuned in to something happening outside the hut. The Flicker looked up toward the curved roof and slowly rose out of a crouch. "They've spotted us," she whispered.

"It is so," Dorsom hissed.

"I must decoy." Natala squatted as if she was gathering her strength, then leapt. In midair, the Flicker appeared to dissolve before Sami's stunned eyes, so her body turned into a stream of purple dust. It whooshed up through a tiny crack in the thatch overhead like a genie escaping a magic lantern.

Dorsom grabbed Sami's arm. "Nixie's soldiers have scented us. We may come under fire. Sami—it's best if you wait here!" Without waiting for an answer, he also squatted, then jumped into a stream of powder, pouring upward and out of the tiny opening.

Sami got to her feet and pushed at the rough walls, but they only shifted and moved around. It was like being trapped inside a woven basket. "I've got to help them!" She pushed on the top of the hut with all her might but couldn't find the opening. "How did I get *in* here?" she cried. "How do I get *out*?"

They brought you through the top opening. The bat's voice scraped into her thoughts. *But Shadow huts reweave and tighten their openings after you come inside.*

The suffocation seemed to close in around her. Sami pounded on the rough, bristling thatch with her hands. "Let me out! I NEED TO GET OUT!"

Wait, Samara. Breathe. The bat's thought cut into her mind. *Stand. Allow.*

The bat's words repeated: *Breathe. Stand.* They slowly worked into her consciousness. *Allow.* Did she know how to do that? Sami wasn't sure if she should even listen. This *was* a Shadow creature, after all—could she trust it? Still, the words circled her own thoughts, splitting them open, making her imagination feel bigger and freer. She realized she didn't have to trust the voice—she could feel the strength of the words herself. Slumped against the thatch, her fists scratched up from the rough edges, Sami put the side of one hand in her mouth and tasted blood. Slowly, her anger and fear subsided. Bit by bit, she grew focused and resolved. She sent her thought to the Shadow bat: *Please, help me. I want to join the others.*

Then stand beneath my voice, it responded.

Sami stood directly beneath one of the tiny slivers of light. About two feet over her head, it looked about the size of a dime.

Now a deep breath. Close the eyes. Steady yourself. Allow yourself to atomize.

Sami frowned. *To—what?* Her shoulders fell. She searched the gloom for the bat. "But I don't know how!"

Its voice returned: *Focus, Samara. Again.*

Sami took another deep breath. She imagined atoms, powder, releasing herself into this form she didn't understand.

Atomize. The image of Dorsom dissolving and whisking up the opening played through her mind, over and over. *Atomize!*

Nothing happened.

She dropped her hands. "It's not working. I can't."

"You will," the bat promised. "If you let yourself." *Again! Focus. Close the eyes. Lift the palms. Breathe. Breathe. Rise, Samara. Rise.*

Shaking her head, Sami screwed her eyes shut again. *Breathe,* she told herself. She could hear her own pulse pounding in her head. It wasn't going to work, she just knew it. *Rise.* This was dumb, totally pointless. *Breathe.* Just totally . . .

Just at the moment of giving up, she realized something actually was happening inside her body. Her hands and feet tingled and a weird scrambling, sparkling feeling began moving from a point within her chest throughout her whole body. Her eyes flew open in alarm. Everything seemed to be turning to powder. The gloomy interior looked like it was covered in fine ash. Her skin looked like ashes. She felt an intense, uncomfortable weight pressing in on every inch of her, her toes and fingers about to pop. Then, all at once, there was delicious, wild release: light air streamed through her skin, her fingers, every part of her.

Everything she was, everything she believed herself to be, poured into smoke, curling into powder, and all was new, ripe, flowing.

Streaming. Seeing and not seeing the world flatten into a corkscrewing ribbon of dark blue. Sami shot forward, through a minute opening in the hut. From that tiny distilled point, her substance returned, arms and head and legs reknitting, growing solid against the ground.

She was almost sorry to feel herself whole again—so heavy and earthbound. But she also felt stronger than before and her mind was clear and sparkling, as if she'd washed it through the sky.

Perhaps she had.

21

After a moment of making sure she was still in one piece, Sami scanned her surroundings. The sun was setting and cast long shadows. But these shadows glittered like opals, so the patterns of palm fronds and rooftops and buildings had a pale bluish glitter. She was standing in an open field, much like the fields around Sami's middle school. She spotted Dorsom first—he was running toward a stand of palm trees and bushes. Natala followed close behind, trailing sparks on the grass.

They weren't running away, she realized. They were trying to attract the attention of something—or someone—to distract it from the hut. The place where her Flicker friends believed she was still hidden.

Sami's eyes felt unusually sharp and her mind blazed through thoughts. She felt as if she were seeing everything at once, the Flickers running, the trees blowing. The nearby roll of the ocean was a saffron-yellow blur with white flecks. The tang of salt air looked lemon yellow, and a gardenia flower glistened like crystals.

There was also, overhead, a kind of motion in the wind and clouds, as if they'd taken on an almost muscular shape. She hadn't noticed before, but it was clear now, growing like a body in the sky, hovering and bending over the Flickers.

Air rushed into her lungs and she started running after the others. "Guys!" she shouted. "I'm out!" She could run faster than before, her feet pounding over the grass. She cried again, "I'm coming!"

Dorsom looked over his shoulder, shock on his face. "How—how on earth did you—?"

"We've gotta get out—it isn't safe here," she shouted.

The clouds rumbled and a bolt of lightning struck the ground. For an instant, brilliance lit everything. But this bolt was illuminated emptiness. Like something tearing the sky.

Natala whirled and held out her hand to Sami.

"Don't stop!" Sami panted. She switched from speaking to thinking without pausing, too breathless to speak: *This way.* In her peripheral vision she saw Dorsom and Natala follow her.

They were in a stretch of open field and sandy rubble and distant houses, and she believed if they could get out of the open area they'd be safer. But before Sami could say anything, another empty bolt slammed the ground behind them. She felt the earth vibrate and she smelled smoke and old rust.

Dorsom caught up to her. *How did you release yourself from the hut?*

I atomized! she thought-shouted. *It was totally cool. I stood under the opening and—* At that moment, another huge bolt struck just in front of them. So close the superdark hurt her eyes. They fell to their knees, ears ringing, ground trembling. Natala, who was just behind, crashed into them.

Sami saw it before she tumbled into it: a second bolt. This one, she knew, hit its target. Every particle inside her body seemed to squeeze and harden, as if she had turned into a gigantic knot. The world disappeared and in its place was a sizzling river. It spun, pulling her in and down, flattening her body, the way she'd flattened when she first went through the mirror. Her mind was gone: instead, there was only a searching intelligence, a spotlight of thought and question, swallowing her whole, sucking her down.

Something trickled across her consciousness. A pale swipe of something. She twisted toward it and felt her spirit rekindle and flame outward.

Gathering herself, Sami focused every bit of her mind. She felt wisps of Natala and Dorsom's voices inside of her. She reached toward those wisps and felt herself gaining energy. Concentrating, giving it everything she didn't know she had, she pushed back, with her thoughts and emotions and will. The memory of her father returned—as powerful and alive as the thought of her mother and grandmother and brother. Everyone she knew and loved was inside of her, fighting with her, gathering within her bones and flesh, all of them helping her to push back.

Once again she felt unbearable pressure—almost as if she were trapped back inside the ground hut, compressing, about to atomize. This time it was even worse. It didn't stop. It was going to kill her.

Then she felt something shimmer under her push.

The glassiness fractured. A million hairline cracks and slivers seemed to fill the air. With a roaring explosion, the pressure shattered, sailing outward in a trillion tiny shards. In its place was the natural darkness of the Silverworld night, nearly bright as day. The sun had set, and the sky was filled with liquid stars and a crescent moon, and Sami was lying flat on her back, staring up at them.

She couldn't hear anything, not the wind or the crickets or the distant thunder. It was silence almost more than silence because, for the first time since she'd gotten to Silverworld, she couldn't hear the thoughts of the Flickers.

The last time she'd heard silence like that was at her father's funeral.

She was four years old, and even though people said you couldn't remember things that happened at such a young age, she remembered that day. The faces of friends and relatives loomed into her vision. Words and sounds bubbled from their mouths, then floated away before they reached her. Tony held her hand tightly while they were swept up in rain clouds of arms and faces and tears. She didn't remember much beyond the impossible strangeness of knowing that her father was inside of the shiny box, that and the wet muffled quiet that surrounded everything, including her own feelings. Only a few words dribbled through and even these were quiet as thoughts: *car; terrible accident; so sudden; so young.*

He was a doctor. He used to say: "A son, a daughter, a doctor, a lawyer, and a grandma! The perfect family." Her father fixed people. Only, for some reason—Sami learned—he couldn't fix himself.

She pieced it together slowly as she got older: He'd been walking across the medical campus, on his way to his office. It was an early morning in the fall—a beautiful time of year in Ithaca. He wasn't paying much attention as he approached the street. He rarely did, Sami knew—her mother said he was the original absentminded professor. But then he saw one of his students walk in front of a car. She was looking down at her phone, texting with friends about a late paper. Joe pushed her out of the way, but he wasn't fast enough to save himself. He died on impact, the ambulance driver said.

The student's parents sent them an enormous wreath and the girl sent them a long tearful letter, telling them how grateful and how sorry she was. She dropped out of school and didn't come to the funeral.

In the end, though, really, it was all a dumb accident. And there was no way to get him back.

When Teta told stories of crossing the desert, she often wove in a mention of a young shaman—a tall, good-looking man, who could heal people with his herbs. In these stories, the young shaman would talk about bravery and determination, about how sometimes you've got to do what you know is right—even when it doesn't feel good at all.

Without the photographs, Sami couldn't quite remember her father's face, but she remembered his smile, the warmth of his arms, and she knew that no matter what, she was never alone.

22

The sky still rumbled and crackled but the lightning appeared to be fading, retreating into a far bank of clouds over the ocean. Shaking and wobbly, Sami sat up. So she was still alive, after all. Her vision seemed clear and her hearing was restored. In fact, her senses were still sharper than ever. She could smell the ocean salt and hear the grass moving in the breeze.

She rolled to her knees, steadied herself, then got to her feet. The fields around her were dark and empty and she experienced a moment of fear that she fought to keep down. Where were the others? She began to slowly scan the scene around her, her eyes taking in every subtle contour and nuance.

Then she noticed something—a glint like a flake of light. Then another. She hurried toward it. There was a series of these flecks and as she approached, she watched them take on the shape of a boy-man lying on his side. It was an outline in dotted light, like a child had traced around him with a gel pen. Heart pounding, Sami squatted next to the dotted outline and put her hand on his. "Dorsom? Oh, please. Please come back. Oh, this is my fault!"

Her eyes filled with tears and the world seemed to tilt. When she noticed a burst of color spreading under her hand, she thought she was seeing things. Then she watched that color swirl forward into his arm, filling in the dotted outline, until Dorsom was lying there, fully formed and solid as ever. A transparent wave seemed to wash through his body and he took a deep breath. His eyes fluttered open, round and luminous in the Silverworld night, and they rested on Sami. He frowned and sat up. "What happened?"

Sami knelt and threw her arms around him. "You're *alive*."

He nodded as they released each other. "Thanks to you!"

"*And* you. I felt you and Natala fighting to help me when I was struck."

He shook his head. "That is what rebalancers do. We tune in to energy. We used ours to help you amplify yours. We helped you narrow your focus to make it stronger."

She sat back, staring at him and the way he seemed to reflect her own expression—as if she were looking in a mirror. "Were we dead?"

He smiled. "We don't draw such clear lines in this World. Not like in yours. We have inside-of-time and outside-of-time. For a smallest while, we were outside-of-time."

"We got hit," Sami muttered. "They zapped us good."

The soldiers. Dorsom nodded, rubbing the back of his neck. "Nixie's army. Their powers grow and grow—exponentially. We've been fighting her Shadow soldiers for a long time, but I've never seen—or felt—any such thing as this. They've seized and channeled storm and electric currents."

Sami ran her hands over her arms, making sure she was still in one piece. Then something occurred to her. "But you know the weird thing? Somehow . . . I didn't feel like they were trying to kill us. More like—like, trap us."

"You, Sami. She needs *you*. You're the key to Crossing between Worlds." Dorsom's face was drawn and serious in the moonlight. "She needs a Silverwalker to open the door between Worlds."

Sami pushed herself up to stand. "Well, she can't have me."

Dorsom studied her in the sparkling moonlight. It had an opal luster and made everything flutter with tiny pink and teal dots. He smiled and nodded. "No, she can't."

They found the dotted outline of Natala in the grass, lying motionless on her side. Sami touched her arm and marveled at the way light and life flashed through her form. The two of them embraced.

"Incredible, Sami! You brought me back." Natala's eyes shone. "You directed breath energies in through me. Your ions—your heat and water vibrations—they recharged me!"

Dorsom nodded, his hands on his hips, and said to Sami, "You are ready."

23

Slipping from her embrace with Natala, Sami noticed something in the night sky. It looked like a bright speck of night breaking away. She stood slowly, alongside the Flickers, staring.

"What do you see?" Dorsom asked.

It flapped again, and all at once, Sami remembered a moment, while trapped inside the Shadow lightning, when an image came to her of a silver string looping through darkness. She'd had no room to think, she'd merely turned in the direction of the string. It had helped her escape from the lightning blast, giving her a trail to follow. "I think it's . . ." She started to walk toward the spiraling.

The flapping moved closer and came into focus. Bobbing over branches, the Shadow bat appeared. "It's you!" Sami rushed forward. "You were back there—inside the ground hut—with me. You showed me how to get out."

The creature was a blur of waxy light and flapping. It gave a series of soft screeches: *And you escaped both hut and lightning beautifully. But now it's time for your next movements. The Shadow creature grows.*

Dorsom nodded, responding, *When Nixie's soldiers struck us, they read us—our thoughts and intentions. Now she knows even more. If we really want to make it to the Castle Shadow, we'll have to begin the journey right away.*

Sami must have time to rest, Natala protested. *She just survived a Shadow blast. Can't we give her a minute to recover?*

There are no extra seconds, the bat thought. *Sami needs must go to the Bare Isles, and the time is now. There's no other way. The Shadows may think they've destroyed you all, but soon they will sense your energies and come hunting again.*

Sami could feel the agitation in the Flickers beside her, a bit like bands of heat rising from the top of a flame. "What are the Bare Isles?" Sami's voice was little more than a whisper.

Dorsom pointed toward the horizon. "A chain of empty islands. They extend over the Eastern waters. Flickers never go there—both out of custom and fear. It's Nixie's domain."

Sami looked at Dorsom and Natala and shook her head. "There's no need for either of you to go any farther. I came to Silverworld to help my grandmother. This is my trip to take. I'll follow the bat as far as it will take me. I won't ask either of you to risk more than you already have."

"Don't you know our answer?" Natala asked with a smile. "Rebalancers won't divide. Ever. We're a team and it won't be easy to get rid of us, I'm afraid."

"Please save discussions for the road!" Dorsom cut in. "We can talk as much as you like if we're also moving."

24

There were no signposts to the Bare Isles, just notches in the sides of grassy tree stumps and an occasional trampled path. Mostly, there was a long swath of dirt and brush and trees bearing fruit that looked like sausages or cats or tiny houses. Dorsom hadn't wanted to wait for sunrise—the journey would take several Silverworld days and nights, he said, and they'd make safer progress under the cover of dark. They'd set off on foot. Horses or camels, Natala had explained, might draw more attention. Wherever there was energy, she'd said, there were Shadows.

It'd been hours since her meal back in the Actual World, and Sami was starting to feel hungry again, when the bat—a creaky blur of wings that circled above—led them to a sprawling bush in the center of a clearing.

"A vapor plant," Natala said, clapping her hands. "Ingenious! Such wondrous fruit."

"What's so ingenious about a bush?" Sami asked. She didn't see anything on it that looked very edible. It was thick, covered with tiny berries like glass beads. "Do you eat these?"

"In a way." Dorsom plucked a handful of berries and dropped some in her hand. They were hard and glittered in the brilliant moonlight. "Put them in your mouth while you think about whatever you'd most like to eat."

"Just so," Natala said. "The berries reflect the thoughts of the one who is eating them. They imitate tastes and smells of remembered foods. You seem to be eating. Though really you aren't," she added.

"There's tiny bits of nutrition in the berry, but mostly they just let you *feel* like you're eating. Child Flickers call these snack trees—what you munch when no true food is around." Dorsom popped a few berries into his mouth and smiled. "Bread, butter, salt! Almost fresh from the table."

Intrigued, Sami sniffed the berries, then cautiously placed one in her mouth. Eyes closed, she began thinking about the crispy falafel sandwiches with tahini sauce that Teta used to make in the days before she stopped speaking.

Then, to Sami's amazement, the taste was right there, on her tongue: the smell of spattering oil, the crunchy, spicy balls, fresh tomatoes, lettuce, creamy tahini sauce, all tucked inside warm pita bread. Hunger sharpened her appetite and she picked berry after berry, filling herself until she thought she'd never need to eat another bite. For a few moments, the flavors brought her back to the round table in their old kitchen where she'd sat beside her mother, teta, brother, and father. Each of them talking and eating and telling stories. The food made the stories better and the stories made the food taste better, her father used to say. Her family was present in the taste of the food, and as she ate the berries, she felt both a sweet joy and a jolt of almost unbearable homesickness.

Natala touched her arm. "It's a comfort feeling, but soon we must find you better food."

Sami and the Flickers filled their pockets with vapor plant berries before setting off again.

25

They walked through that night, and the following days, sleeping and waking with the movements of the sun, snacking on vapor berries and whatever fruits and roots the Flickers could forage (though none, Sami thought, tasted as wonderful as vapor plant berries). The bat easily flapped and glided over their heads and roosted in the trees, and neither of the Flickers looked any worse for sleeping outside on the sandy ground all night. In fact, even though she was hungry, Sami was surprised at how good and rested she felt. It was like Silverworld somehow didn't make the same physical demands on its inhabitants— everything was softer, lighter, easier.

She also felt the vigilance of her companions, their gaze continually sweeping and scanning the landscape as they walked. Occasionally, they passed other Flickers—usually traveling alone, wrapped head to toe, only their hands and faces showing. The women wore heavy black bangles on their wrists and jingling chains across their foreheads. The men had covered all but their eyes, which glimmered, surrounded by golden tattoos. Sometimes Sami felt their thoughts and curiosity bend toward her, and she became increasingly adept at closing her own mind and staying silent.

On their fourth day of travel, they encountered a small caravan: a woman led the way, trailed by two men and four children. The men both had babies wrapped against their chests in soft slings. They were leading a row of grunting burgundy camels, who peered at Sami, their sides glistening as if rubbed with oils.

The woman's head was uncovered, except for a chain of silver coins draped across her forehead, down behind her ears, then curved forward to lie flat on her chest. Her skin was a deep woodlands green and her long hair was a sheet of darker green silk. She wore a cutlass strapped to her hip and a dagger bound to her ankle. As the caravan approached, Dorsom and Natala drew closer to Sami, and the bat veered off into the trees. *Better not to mix with such as these,* the small creature thought. *I have an instinct.* Sami noticed what looked like a collection of small animal skulls—of sheep or goats possibly—tied in a clicking bundle to one of the camel saddles.

"Flesh-eaters," Natala murmured to Sami, eyes averted. "Let's keep walking."

But the group slowed as the woman studied them—Sami in particular—and there was no way to avoid conversation. "Flickers," she said, "need thee water or provision? Art thou lost?"

"We are well. We are grateful for your concern," Dorsom said quietly.

"Then know thou that this is the approach to the Dominion of the Bare Isles and Castle Shadow of the Bleak Fairy Nixie?"

"Aware we are," Dorsom said. "That is our course."

Once again, Sami felt the woman's scrutiny. "And how is it," she said at last, "that I hear not this young one's thoughts?"

Dorsom placed one hand on Sami's shoulder and the woman lifted her eyebrows. "She is unused to strangers," he murmured.

"Strange, though. Thy thoughts I perceive well enough. But this one . . ." She squinted, moving closer to Sami, who instinctively dropped her eyes. "Stunted is she?"

"In no way is she stunted," Natala said indignantly. "She is restrained."

The woman began to circle her and Sami felt sweat break out on her temples and palms. "Or is she a captive? Another prisoner to be delivered to the Bleak Fairy?" Sami noticed the woman's hand move toward her knife as one man shuffled backward with the children. "Mean thou to sell or enslave her?" she asked evenly.

"Rebalancers we are!" Dorsom retorted.

The woman's head lifted sharply. "Thy laws of balancement mean nothing to me," she uttered. "Such beings as you care only for your World of colors and regulation. You leave all others at the mercy of the Nixie forces, to dwindle away in her cages."

Sami noticed the other man pass his sleeping infant to the first man. In a single movement, he turned, seizing and unsheathing a sword that had been lashed to the side of a camel.

Instantly, Dorsom pulled a cutlass from his satchel. "Wait, no!" Sami cried, too late. The woman sprang at Dorsom, swinging her large blade. Dorsom parried it, pushing her away, but she leapt back easily. The man at her side clumsily slashed out with his sword. Natala pulled Sami out of the fray, then grabbed the man's arm.

The woman clashed knives with Dorsom and they fell on their sides, rolling in the sand. She had remarkable strength and agility and she fought intensely, striking blade against blade, until at last Dorsom fell back. She pinned him on the ground with one hand and held the blade of her knife at his throat with the other. But suddenly his eyes widened and he blurted, "But you are not Flicker?"

Sami jumped up and backhanded the sword out of the man's grip. Natala pushed him to the ground and jumped onto his chest, restraining him with her hands and knees—a small dagger in one of her hands.

"No!" cried the woman. "Thou mustn't hurt him!"

Sami turned to see the woman's green skin briefly flash dark and transparent, and she had a sudden understanding. "She's—a Shadow?"

The woman looked at Sami. Like that, the color drained from her skin and hair, and she flattened into the silhouette of a woman, a perfect paper cutout. "Thou art *Actual*," she breathed, rising and letting Dorsom get to his feet. Natala backed off the man slowly. "Such dreams as never I dreamed," the Shadow marveled, walking to Sami. "I thought I was imagining such."

She lifted Sami's wrist in her cutout palm, turning it. "Heavy, dense," she said approvingly. "Strong. How many times I've wondered how 'twould be to meet an Actual One."

Sami pulled away. "I'm not a captive. No more than *you* are a Flicker!"

She saw a ripple go through the murky form. "Much of our World thou dost not understand, child. I travel in Flicker guise to remain with my family."

Sami frowned in confusion and Natala said gently, "She shape-shifts. It takes a lot of skill and energy for a Shadow to imitate a Flicker, but it can be done."

"But why do it?" Sami asked.

"Rules of Balancement state that Flicker and Shadow must not cohabit," Dorsom explained. "Eons ago it was written, long before our time."

The woman's shape nodded. "'Twas my double misfortune— first, to fall for a charming man-Flicker at the marketplace." She gestured to the glowering man holding the sword. "And second, to succumb to another handsome face at the baths." She gestured to the Flicker with the children. "My offspring are half-Flick, half-Shade—unacceptable to all society. Eternally in movement and in hiding are we." Her shape twisted toward the bundled forms hiding behind the camels, then turned back. Sami could make out a sort of glint on her silhouette that might have been a smile. "But please, let us speak not of grief. We invite all to take coffee and such things as an Actual might wish to eat. Guests of the caravan thou shalt be."

26

The Shadow traveler, whose name was Lamida, and her two Flicker husbands, Yazar and Tajreef, quickly assembled a small camp, setting up coral-colored tents, spreading rugs, pulling blankets, cushions, and food from their provisions. Sami was put in a place of honor near the food and Tajreef offered her the coffee first. If this had been the Actual World, she reflected, she would never have tried it—it looked so thick and dark as he poured it in a stream from the lifted spout into a doll-sized cup. It reminded her of the cups of coffee, *cafecitos*, that she saw people sipping at the Cuban market at home. But it tasted earthy and delicious and didn't seem to vanish in her throat. Sami drank two cups before Natala touched her wrist and murmured, "This is strong stuff."

Sami was curious about this family with two husbands. The

Flicker men set out platters of pink grapes and yellow bread, and they whispered to each other as they worked, shooting narrow looks at Sami and her friends. Lamida was equally curious about Sami. Reclining on embroidered red cushions beside her guests, she said, "So many years of gazing into the Silverskinned, yet I never imagined I'd see an Actual in person! How comest thou to the Silverworld, child?"

Fingering the tiny cup, Sami said, "Well, some have said I was tricked or . . . lured, I guess, through the mirror. But it was my idea first to read these special words from my grandmother's spell book. It's strange. I feel like I still don't have the whole story."

The Flicker men murmured to each other and nudged the curious children away from Sami.

Lamida lifted her chin in the way Sami's grandmother used to when she was annoyed. "Superstitious my husbands are, fearful and weak." She sighed. "They see the Shadow mark on thee."

Sami frowned in confusion. When she turned, both Dorsom and Natala dropped their eyes. *We may have neglected to mention . . .* Dorsom's thought was low as a whisper. *When you were hit by Shadow fire—they leave a sort of—mark. Here.* He pointed to the top of his own forehead.

Sami touched her hairline, but could feel nothing. He shook his head. *It's visible only to Shadows. And those who live among them and know their ways.*

"It helps Shadows to identify prey," Lamida said with a shrug. "Though usually the mark is just used on other Shadows. As shape-shifters, they are harder to track. And to be sure, most hunted Flickers never survive a Shadow strike, anyway—not of the magnitude that hit you."

"They're hunting me?" Sami asked in alarm—though suddenly she knew they were, of course. Hadn't she sensed them lurking, sniffing for her, throughout the long journey to the Bare Isles?

The men turned skewers with bits of meat over a small central fire, filling the air with a spicy, delectable scent that reminded Sami of lakeside picnics and her grandmother's shish kabobs. Dorsom and Natala politely declined the plates of sizzling morsels. Sami swallowed hard and, after a moment, also said no to the food.

"Child Actual!" Lamida held out a kabob in a bit of bread. "Be tainted not by squeamish Flicker customs. All my children and both my Flicker-men now enjoy the nourishment of meats—praise to the Goddess for her bounty. Some die that others may live. 'Tis the circle of life."

Sami pressed her lips together, then muttered, "Well, I guess. As the honored guest, I don't want to offend anyone...." With the Flickers watching, Sami accepted the bite of food and ate. It tasted exactly like grilled lamb, and it was so good in the fresh air, after she'd gone so long without solid food, it nearly brought tears to her eyes. Best of all, while it was lighter than Actual food, it didn't seem to disappear when she swallowed. Sami sat beside the crackling green-gold fire and told Lamida and the others about her grandmother's worsening health and her journey through Silverworld. She was filled with home-sickness as she spoke. She missed everything: their house, her bedroom, even Florida: the pink hibiscus flowers, the sweet-scented gardenias, the fresh water from a coconut. Now the embers crackled and whirled green sparks in the chilly darkness, and Sami soon realized she had finished off nearly the whole platter while Dorsom and Natala had discreetly looked away.

As Sami and the adults ate and talked, the children peered at the visitors from behind their glowering fathers. Three of the children looked like Flickers, though Sami noticed their eyes were unusually wide and black and their skin almost translucent, so she could see the shadows of things behind them. The youngest child looked exactly like a Shadow except for one detail—a pair of startling, lavender-colored, violet-lashed eyes floating in her silhouette face.

The child was, Sami thought, lovely in an entirely new way. She stared at Sami, sneaking out from behind one of her fathers, gazing up at her.

What is your name? Sami thought-asked.

After a long pause, the child whispered, *Yamay.*

Frowning, both of the husbands jumped up, grabbed the children, and shuffled them back into a tent.

Lamida chuckled. "She thinks thou'rt like her."

"Me?" Sami felt both pleased and confused. "What do you mean? In what way?"

An embarrassed hush fell over the group. The Shadow shrugged and said finally, "Mixed. A little of both things."

"Mixed?" She looked quizzically after the child, then murmured, "I did always feel kind of different, like, from the rest of my family. Like the oddball."

"Now that thou'rt in Silverworld," Lamida said softly, "knowest thou why?"

"Why I feel that way?" Sami sighed and faced into the wind. Yamay was perhaps five years younger than her, but at that moment Sami felt like she was a hundred years older. She knew she didn't appear so visibly different from others, the way that Yamay did—yet there was something inside her that had always felt out of place. Her mother had said it was her will; Teta said it was her power.

"I don't know," she finally admitted. "But I do feel like I'm getting closer."

Lamida put her hand on Sami's shin and Sami had to stifle a gasp—it looked as if there was a hand-shaped hole in her leg. Perhaps sensing Sami's fright, Lamida removed her hand, and Sami's leg looked whole again. The husbands cleared away all traces of cooking, then withdrew into their tents, muttering to each other and casting their angry glances, their words and thoughts rattling in the distance like threats.

The Flickers wanted to get back on the road, but Sami felt drowsy after the big meal and the weather was increasingly rough. Palm fronds lashed the air over their heads and sand stung their skin. Lamida insisted they spend the night with the caravan before making their final approach to the Bare Isles. "Bats and Yellow Eyes, Fangles and carrion birds prey all about this region," the Shadow warned. "And perhaps there are worse still where thou'rt headed. Best to remain with us tonight—we understand the Night Creatures."

"Have you been to the Bare Isles?" Natala asked.

The Shadow shook her head quickly. "Never. And never will I! Legends are many and realities even worse."

Early the next morning, Sami found Yamay sleeping next to her on the blanket, her cutout of a body just as warm and solid as any child's. Still drowsing, she smiled and snuggled closer to the Shadow child, only to feel an icy darkness fall over her face. Sami turned and gasped: one of the Flicker husbands was standing over her with a curved white dagger. His eyes widened and he lifted the knife. Sami jumped up and knocked it from his hand. That instant, the other husband grabbed her from behind. With a cry, Sami seized his wrist and arm, instinctively swinging down, and flipped him over her back. He landed with a thud on top of the first husband.

Then Lamida and the Flickers were there, shouting. Lamida screamed at her husbands, stomping on the knife and breaking the blade. Yamay ran crying to her brothers and sisters. While Natala checked Sami to make sure she was unharmed, Lamida returned to apologize. "They are like children, those two. Worse than children, in truth. Tajreef believed 'twould be best to sacrifice thee now to spare thee from horrors to come of the Nixie."

Dorsom snapped, "Better we take our chances with the Nixie! It is well time for us to be on our way."

But the Shadow pleaded for them to wait just one second longer. "I would try to convince thee to abandon this journey, Flickers." She pointed toward the sunrise, where Sami noticed odd, pencil-thin lines dancing in the distance, like a kind of straight gray lightning. "Closer they come on thy scent. And thine approach to the Bare Isles—it's too direct, too open to her sentries." She drew in the sand with a stick, then pointed, saying, "Here. This spot is little known and rarely used. This may give some advantage."

Then she turned to Sami. Her chain of coins outlined her face so it was almost possible for Sami to discern the Shadow's features. "Yamay is tenderest to mine heart," she confided in a low voice. "So hurt and unhappy she is never to find one like herself. Yet for this day and night thou hast made her happy. For such relief, Silverwalker, a special gift I have." From one of the pouches in a camel saddle, she removed a translucent paper folded into a slim envelope, much like the golden paper star Sami had found in her pocket back in the Actual World. Handing it to Sami, she said, "Here thou shalt find my spell most powerful. 'Tis powder of revealing and unbinding. And most illegal, to be sure, here in Silverworld," she added with a wink at Dorsom and Natala. "Its crystals are poisonous. Never lose or let go. Only once shall it work. Someday, thou might be in need of such stuff."

Sami accepted the gift with thanks as the other Flickers quickly loaded their satchels with provisions from the caravan. As they set out, Sami felt the pressure of a strong hug around her middle. "I thou shalt see again," she heard Yamay whisper, a pair of lavender eyelids pressed to her chest. Sami looked down into outer space darkness in the shape of a little girl, a single star twinkling at her center.

27

After another windy day and stormy evening of walking, Sami realized they were again approaching the beach. They were headed to the hidden route Lamida had described, winding over seagrasses and between dunes. The sand, kicking up in whirlwinds, looked gauzy in the sunrise.

This was a new place, a new land. There were streaks of black and gold in the morning sky, and Sami could hear the songs of strange birds with deep voices like flutes. In the distance, rising above the waves, she could see a landmass—the first of the Bare Isles, Natala told her.

Also, past the edge of the sand and surf, she could make out some sort of towering shape. She studied it for a few moments until gradually her eyes focused: it was a woman. Ten stories high, rising straight out of the water. The gigantic grayish-white statue rose eerily, impossibly before them. It stood in the water on wide-apart legs rising into a long waist and broad shoulders; there was a fan of wild hair that pointed and curled in every direction, and its arms were held above its head, fingers splayed. Sami stared at it without blinking, half expecting it to break out of its frozen stance at any moment and seize them.

"Wow," she breathed.

"The Stone Keeper, I believe it's called," Dorsom murmured. "Nixie created it long ago, to frighten away intruders from the hidden route."

"It works," she said.

"I've heard stories of this creation," Natala said with the faintest smile. "And scarce believed it existed."

"Are you positive we should go this way?" Sami asked. "What if Lamida was tricking us? Maybe this is a trap. . . ." She gulped. She was still trying to figure out Silverworld, who and what to trust. And things seemed even stranger and less familiar out here in the Bare Isles. On the horizon, the bronze-colored half sun had a slightly fizzy edge, as if someone had dropped it in a soda.

Dorsom smiled and said, "That is, to be sure, a risk we must take. But I do promise, this is only a statue. A big one. Having its intended effect on you." He brushed hair out of his eyes and frowned; Sami saw his anxious expression clearly in the sparkling light. "Unfortunately, a statue is the least of our worries."

The morning was turning hot, but Sami was the last to wade into the cool surf. She'd never liked going into the ocean, and she had to close her eyes and take deep breaths as she inched forward into the water. A big surge nearly knocked her over and her eyes flew open to see the enormous bronze legs and crashing waves. Sunlight glinted off its metallic lips, its wide, wild eyes, its outflung arms. It looked lit up, *alive*, just as if it were marching through the waves about to snatch her up. She shivered and looked away.

The water itself seemed ominous here, very different from the water at the pier. Though it was a brilliantly sunny morning, this water was streaked with deep navy, and cobalt currents. The waves slithered and hissed and whispered, and it seemed she heard voices in them, murmuring to her.

The ocean had always scared Sami. Growing up in the middle of New York State, she hadn't had that many chances to go to the beach or to practice swimming. She took ice-skating lessons and knew how to ski and hike and snowshoe. But none of that did her any good when she got into big, wild waves.

And she didn't like the way she couldn't see what was under the surface. There were always things brushing against her in the open water or curling under her toes. Just seaweed, her mom reassured her on their vacations to Lake Ontario or Jones Beach—maybe a curious fish or two. But it was creepy getting touched by stuff she couldn't make out. The one time she'd put on a mask and looked under the water, she'd spotted an enormous fish right next to her leg, and had run straight back to land.

"Does anyone else hear what I hear?" Now Sami stopped in the foaming surf, the wind rumpling her hair.

Dorsom and Natala slid a look at each other. "What is what?" Dorsom asked. "What do you perceive?"

Sami frowned and shook her head, listening; it was hard to pick up anything clearly above the pounding of her heart. "It's quiet, but . . . I swear, it sounds like—questions. You don't hear that?" The murmurs seemed to rise directly out of the water, as if thousands of invisible swimmers were all speaking at once. Their voices weren't quite thoughts or audible sounds, but some whirling middle range that echoed through her head and reminded her of her grandmother's stories of the spinning dervishes.

You can't do this.
Who do you think you are?
You're scared.
Why are you doing this?
You won't survive.

Over and over, the challenges rose from each ripple so her chest tightened and she backed away on the sand, hands clasped over her ears.

Dorsom frowned. "Shadow voices in the water—they snag oddments and fragments of your own thoughts and use them to bedevil and frighten you."

Natala took Sami's arm. "Waterborne Shadows. They're refracting—bending your mind. Water amplifies thought. It's a way to use information from you, against you."

"The stiller you can settle in your mind, the better," Dorsom urged. "Make your mind as quieted as possible."

"But how? The ocean is, like, my biggest fear—I really *am* scared!" Sami wailed, and, almost as if they were listening, the unseeable Shadow swimmers surged back with hundreds more thoughts:

How can you . . . ?
Why would you . . . ?
You mustn't . . .

"It's all right to be afraid." Dorsom's eyes gleamed. He stood directly in front of her, the sun washing across their faces. "Now, let your mind hold its breath, Sami."

She opened her mouth, about to tell him what a terrible idea that was, when he held up his hand. "Please, just *allow*. Let your mind hold its breath," he repeated. "Only try it."

Sami stared at him, then nodded slowly. "I'll try." Like so many things in Silverworld, it made no sense to her, but she just told herself, *Hold your breath.* For a moment, she tried actually holding her breath, then gently released it. She blinked slowly. And it seemed as if she began to slow down, and the world around her also slowed. The wind seemed lazier and the water softer.

The strait seemed to turn into the clear warm water of Coconut Shores and, in turn, she felt her heart expanding. She heard seagulls cry out from high overhead, her mother and brother calling to her to come swim.

Sami realized then the water-thoughts had hesitated as well. She tried telling herself: *Go still.* She didn't think about anything except the word *still, still, still,* her eyes following the path of a bird flying big soft circles in the distance. The image of a single spinning dervish came back to her, conjured straight from one of Teta's stories, white robes fanning out, head tipped back toward heaven, face filled with peace.

"Good," Dorsom murmured. "Perfect, actually."

"I think," Natala said quietly, "we haven't time to waste. The way is clear *for now.* Let's make our crossing."

Dorsom held Sami's gaze. "This you can do. Keep your mind soft. We needs must walk the water to get to the Bare Isles. But the greatest importance is to keep your thoughts quiet. Soft-minded."

Sami nodded, not wanting to speak and break her own spell. He lifted his chin, then took one of her hands, and Natala held the other, and together, they entered the deeper water.

In her mind, the image of the dervish kept spinning: she watched as if it were turning in the sky within the path of the distant circling bird. And trying with all her might, Sami didn't let herself remember that she was terrified of the water.

28

Chills prickled Sami's spine as she walked deeper. The water felt cooler and somehow lighter than in the Actual World. *For Teta,* she told herself. She held tightly to Dorsom and Natala, until she was up to her waist. Slowly, she let her eyelids lift. Just beyond the Flickers, a great pair of bronze kneecaps rose out of the ocean and soared into thighs, with the dark bell of the statue's skirt forty-five feet over their heads. Now Sami could make out purple barnacles and seaweed on the metallic surface, covering its cold features—its chiseled brow, curling lips, and hard, blank eyes. It looked cruel and beautiful. "Is—is—that *her?*" she asked. "What the Nixie looks like?"

Dorsom shaded his eyes and looked up. "No knowing. No Flicker's ever seen the actual *her.*"

Natala looked up as well. "There's no telling her native form. Shadows are remarkable shape-shifters."

Sami thought of Lamida in her Shadow form, yet covered in so much jewelry and so many scarves, as if to define her form for the Flickers. She remembered the depthless Shadow full of stars she'd seen bowing before the Rotifer—lovely yet somehow amorphous—like the cosmos itself, capable of becoming anything at any time.

The ocean water swelled and surged around them, knocking them back and forth. Stumbling, Sami couldn't help stealing glances at the statue's cold facade, its swirling hair and outstretched fingers. Suddenly, she thought she saw the thing's mouth curve into a smile and a voice like a lullaby rang through her head: *Come to me!*

Sami cried out, frozen in fear. The two Flickers swiveled toward her as she realized the ocean water had turned gray. It looked to her as if their lower halves had been sheared away by a gray mirror. In an instant, all the whispering questions were back, battering at her mind. "No, no." She released their hands in terror, lurching backward, staggering in the water.

"Don't let them in!" Natala cried.

It was too late. Sami twisted, looking for the beach, but it wasn't there. No matter which way she looked, all she saw was inky water.

"It's an illusion," Dorsom said, coming toward her. "Don't believe it."

Voices hissed through her mind. Now they were asking: *How can you stand this? What are you doing? Why are you here?* She felt things brushing against her legs—it felt like hands, fingers feathering, curling against her, and she shrieked, flailing and trying to pull away.

"Attend me, Sami!" Dorsom commanded. He grabbed her arms and moved directly in front of her. "You can do this. You must. We're halfway there. Keep your eyes to mine. Don't look away. Don't look at or listen to anything but me. Do you understand?"

She was gasping and trembling from the invisible hands, but Dorsom laced his fingers with hers and she managed to nod.

"Come, then! Step upon step. Steady yourself. Breathe. You are fine. Most excellent."

She nodded again and dared a step, though it was like walking into a thicket of sweeping touches. Again Sami gasped, but she didn't look away from Dorsom. She lifted her hands and took hold of his elbows as he held her upper arms. It was a tense dance, moving in a slow line, wobbling through the waves. Gradually, her awareness of the world around her began to diminish. She barely registered when they passed under the cold shadow of the statue's legs. The water crept up to her waist, then her shoulders, but she kept her focus locked on Dorsom.

Staring into his eyes was like looking into one of those images of mirrors inside mirrors. Sami had a vague sense of falling forward and of being drawn forward. He kept murmuring to her and to Sami it felt as if her anxiety were gradually being pulled from her chest—a long rope attached to the string of his voice. *For Teta*, she reminded herself again. *This is for her.* She imagined her brave twelve-year-old grandmother standing up to the desert raiders, bringing them to a halt with a single spell.

Another memory came to her at that moment, of being the smallest child, sitting at the table with her mother, brother, father, grandmother. The world complete at their round table. She knew, though, there was a sadness in her mother. None of the others seemed to notice—at least not her father or brother— Alia was very good at hiding it even from herself. But Sami noticed—every time she complained about the cold climate of New York State, America's lack of sophistication, the fact that no one read, that families split apart, that people spoke only one language. Once, after cracking some eggs for breakfast, Alia shook her head and murmured, "The yolks here are so pale."

Sami knew—her mother compared it all, unfavorably, eternally, to Lebanon.

Yet she rarely spoke of her home country. It was like the most beautiful secret that belonged only to her. Like, if she talked about it too much, it might dissolve and blow away.

Sami used to wish it would.

Now, though, standing waist-deep, facing her greatest fear, Sami realized her mother had also gone on a journey she hadn't planned on—a rather scary and unexpected adventure. She loved her young husband, but she missed her home country so much, and the fighting in Beirut made it seem impossible to return. And now Sami too had, perhaps, a taste of what that might have been like. It was terrible. Shocking. And yet, as she walked through the mysterious waters under the statue, she thought of something Teta had liked to tell her: *Don't let your fears run your life. Don't let them make it smaller.*

Gradually, the hissing voices started to subside. Sami felt the water grow warmer and calmer as they approached a new shore. She let herself dare break eye contact with Dorsom and glanced back at the statue. Its perfect silhouette, carved right out of the sky, seemed to be holding its breath.

The only way out, she reminded herself, *is through.*

29

"...more carrion birds," Natala was saying.

Sami opened one eye, then the other. She was lying curled on her side on the tangerine sand. They were in some sort of bower protected by rich blue palms, the fronds big, lobe-shaped, and flattened. Sunlight spilled through the wide fans and turned everything turquoise. After they'd made it across the Bare Straits, she'd lain down for a few moments once they'd come to this quiet little spot and fallen into a half sleep. Thoughts and sensations coursed through her body, a jumble of relief, emotional exhaustion, and curiosity over whatever was to come. The air was thick and damp, and she felt a pang of hunger. "What were you saying?" She pushed herself up. "Some kind of birds?"

"I didn't realize you were listening." Natala looked abashed. Sami could hear some sort of bird cry now: a hard, prehistoric-sounding echo that rose in waves over the horizon. Darkness appeared to rise as well, like bands of heat over the distant water. Everything was getting darker.

Dorsom nodded. He was sitting with his elbows resting on his bent knees. "Shadow eaters, those birds. They clean up bits of—debris—the Shadow creatures leave behind."

"Bits of *debris?*"

He pointed toward the sky, where there was a lot of bird activity. Sami watched the bending, rippling flight, but when she looked more closely, it seemed she was seeing single wings only—perhaps a bit of tail feather—rising and falling through the air, without need of heads or bodies.

"How do they *do* that? Are those real birds?"

Natala wrapped her forearms around her knees and folded her tattooed hands. It was much hotter on the island and she'd discarded her veil. "Carrion birds sweep up the leavings. Part of the biological systems."

At first there were dozens of the winged things, then there were hundreds, flapping and spiraling through the sky, descending with screams. Sami watched as the weird part-birds swept downward along the palm trees. They skimmed just above the ground, whisking up all sorts of odds and ends—rocks and knobs and roots. Then she seemed to catch the tiny shriek of some small creature snatched in the collecting wings.

Sami leapt to her feet. "They're killing little animals! We have to stop them—they're horrible."

Natala grabbed Sami's arm. "We mustn't interfere. They're part of the ecosystem of the Bare Isles. This is how Shadows clear their environment."

Before Sami could respond she heard a snickering hiss: the flying wings shivered and a whinnying motion filled the air near Sami. The movement appeared to concentrate, lengthen into a slot, then a crossbar, then unrolled into a woman with cascading bubbles of silver-blue hair, amber-brown skin, and glowing gray eyes.

"Shadow bat!" Natala got to her feet.

"Why are you following us?" Dorsom scrambled up to stand beside Sami.

Sami gaped at the lovely young woman with lips like a scarlet slash. "*You're* the bat?"

The woman laughed and combed her fingers along her part, then tossed a few locks of hair behind one shoulder. "I can assume any form I please. Often this amber creature I am. I enjoy the light. Why should the Flickers have all the charm? They're stupid and unsubtle and undeserving." Her eyes glittered with amusement and she put her hands on her hips. She wore a long blue tunic and looked like a pharaonic queen. Outlined with black winged makeup, her eyes were too large for her face, which tapered to a small foxlike chin, and her teeth looked very white and rather sharp. "But I am concerned for you," she said, nodding at Sami. "There are few Silverwalkers indeed, and it worries me how these Flickers enstumble you along, with little sense of the Shadow soldiers."

"How dare you make such accusation?" Natala asked at the same time Dorsom said, "What are you saying?"

The young woman shrugged and gestured to the gray lines shooting from the clouds to the horizon—which Sami had noticed were increasing in size and frequency. "They close in—from all sides. If you want to avoid her sentries, you'll need a guide."

Natala snorted and looked away, but Dorsom thought, *There may be some sense in this.*

"You'll not survive without me," the bat said casually while studying her nails—which, Sami noticed, sparkled with opaline brilliance. "*Nixie's* dimension you're in now—not Silverworld, Flicker-sweet and light."

Dorsom frowned. "I believe Nixie shall not harm Sami." He glanced at Sami and said carefully, "We think she means to make of her a trophy. A prize."

"Very possibly—and yet quite mad is Nixie," the woman shot back. "She wants *and* wants not the Silverwalker. The queen needs must have Samara, yet she's an inconvenient need. And certainly she will not hesitate to dispose of you others."

Dorsom raised his eyebrows at Natala.

I don't like it. Natala's thought was low and unhappy.

Sami stepped in discreetly and said, "I believe our friend will help us—won't you?"

"Bat you may call me," the woman said. "And *you* shall I help, Samara, and alone you." With that, she swept off, her long tunic curling behind her like an ocean crest. "Do try to keep up," she called back over one shoulder. "If you prefer not to be live-swallowed!"

30

Dorsom and Natala kept squinting and scanning the trees, on the alert for anything that looked as if it might seize or eat them. Bat told them she was willing to lead the group as far as she could go, but there would come a point she could go no farther. "Nixie will make gloves from my wings if I am discovered helping your cabal," she hissed.

They set out on their journey on foot once again, crossing the sandy, palm-lined paths of one isle, then marching across shallower water to the next. Bat led the way on a difficult, veering course that avoided what looked like smooth footpaths and cut through dense, pastel-tinted bushes. Sami's thoughts kept returning to Teta and her mother and Tony. The last time she and Tony had talked, they'd had that dumb fight, when she'd accused him of trying to act too grown-up. Now she wished she could take it back, tell him she'd just been so worried about Teta but that was no reason for her to say mean things. She wished they could just go fishing. Or surfing. She wondered what they were doing now, if they had realized yet that she was missing, if they were frantic. She glanced at Dorsom and he shook his head. Startled, she stopped for a moment and laughed. She would never get used to thought-sharing. "Did you hear what I was thinking just now?"

"Possibly—some snippets and snappets might have through-come." He shrugged lightly. "There are at least twenty charted levels of thought in Silverworld—though probably many more—from the lightest and easiest to read to the deepest and most personal. Unimagined even to the self. And I can assure you that back in the Actual World, scarcely minutes have passed since you came to ours. A Silver year is an Actual week."

"So they may not have noticed yet . . . ," she said uncertainly. It was beginning to feel to Sami like she'd been away for a year, not a few Silverworld days.

Dorsom frowned at his feet sweeping through the long brush and grass as they walked. This second, smaller island was dense with tropical foliage and all sorts of odd bird peeps and fantastical colors winking between the palm fronds. Except for the wandering paths of turquoise sands and glints of birdcages in the trees, it seemed almost uninhabited. Yet, even with all this color, she noticed the light was starting to look denser, deeper, the edges of things outlined in increasingly stark lines. The sky overhead seemed gloomier. She wondered if this was true only in Shadow lands, or if indeed the darkness was spreading all over Silverworld.

The deeper they pressed into the Bare Isles, the less anyone spoke. Yellow glints shone in the overgrowth, and sometimes jagged, wild laughter erupted from the bushes. Dorsom kept a hand on his knife at all times: Sami knew he was watching for the wild things Lamida had warned them of. They swished through feathery sea-green blades growing straight out of the ground. They pushed aside branches draped with blossoms like golden spheres or sugar cones or lilac bells. On the next isle, tiny animals peeped at them from the branches; they looked like fur-covered snowballs with round eyes and tiny mouths, and they clucked and chortled and giggled as Sami and the Flickers passed underneath.

"This doesn't seem that scary and terrible," she whispered to Natala.

Natala's lilac brows lifted. "Don't be deceived," she murmured. "Shadow Nixie is a queen of illusion. These islands she arranged to suit her own purposes."

"Enthrall and enfuddle she will," Bat confirmed. She turned to face them yet kept walking backward as easily and naturally as she walked forward. "The more she can mystify her prey, the easier to capture they are."

"Are we walking right into a trap, then?" Sami stared into the woman's gray eyes and felt a kind of pull that made her feel, once again, off-balance—the way so many things did in this world.

"I know not. But no other way is there," Bat said gravely.

Gradually, the wind calmed and the sun grew a bit brighter. Soft pale-pink light washed over the trees and there was a stillness in the air. "I think we've lost them—the Shadow soldiers," Sami said, looking around. "Those Shadow strikes—I don't see them on the horizon anymore."

Shading her eyes, Bat nodded. "They no longer have to chase us."

"They've got us where they want us," Dorsom agreed grimly.

On the other hand, Sami wondered if she and the Flickers still needed to be quite so cautious. But when she considered taking a footpath of lilac stones instead of scaling yet another rough hedge, Bat's thought flew at her: *'Tis a fine way, except for sinking into its cook-hole of quicksilver sand.*

When she eyed a dry trail around a marshy thicket, Bat admonished, *All well if you don't mind being eaten by that herd of razor-toothed leapers.*

After a long afternoon of hiking, climbing, and warnings, Bat stopped them by a switching stand of trees with thick olive-colored leaves. The narrow trunks rubbed against each other, making a squeaking, grunting sound, and the leaves rose and twitched, buoyant and alive.

"What is such place?" Dorsom frowned, scanning their surroundings. Sami was hungry again from all the walking, plus she was sticky with sweat, her feet ached, and her back was sore. She hoped for some more vapor berries as well as a place to sit and put up her feet.

"Wait!" The woman threw out her arms. Sami saw her pupils slide into slits and her body seemed to clap into itself, like a bursting bubble. Suddenly there was a frantic flapping, and Bat chittered above the treetops. Light spangled off its wings so it looked like a piece of wax paper, crumpling and tumbling through the air. After a few moments, the bat returned, light folding into a slit, expanding into a woman.

"'Tis a gazing pool," she said, running her hands over her silver-blue hair. "Go around we should, if we—"

"No. No, it's nearly sun-wane. We need to find a place to stop and rest," Natala said, shaking her head. "And to scavenge more food for Sami."

"This isn't a *Flicker* gazing pool," Bat said, her face furrowed with concern. "To Bare Isles this belongs. . . ."

"We're well aware of that," Dorsom responded. He stretched his arms and shoulders. "But Sami is not a Flicker, much less a trained rebalancer. She's exhausted—we needs must stop!"

Bat's face turned blank and cold, her small mouth getting even smaller. "As you like!" she said with a sniff, then pulled aside a narrow opening in the thin trees, bending them easily, a curtain of blue foliage gathered in her arm. The tree leaves made a hushed, serpentine hiss as the group passed through. Velvety, trimmed grass rolled down to an oval pool; the water was flat and still as a mirror.

As they approached the water, Sami realized the pool was ringed with aquamarine- and jade-colored gems, each about the size of a dinner plate, embedded in the ledge. Up on the lawn,

163

placed like rays around the perimeter of the water, were raised rectangular platforms, about waist-high. Each of the platforms had a canopy of sheer fabric radiant with late-afternoon light as it floated on the breeze.

"Oh, just—wow." Sami went up to one of the platforms and touched the fabric: it was shot through with silver threads. "I wish my mom could see this! And Teta. And even Tony would love this. I mean—it looks like a vacation on some dreamy, far-away island."

"Dreamy, yes," Dorsom murmured. The Flickers followed Sami, gazing around warily. "And not very real."

"Well, it is lovely," Natala conceded. "Whatever it is."

"Take care, Silverwalker," Bat cautioned as Sami moved inside the white canopy, touching the fabric with her finger-tips. "You don't know this place and you mustn't let down your guard inside the Bare Isles."

Enchanted, Sami scarcely heard what the others were say-ing. Inside the white curtains it smelled of fresh rain and ocean mist. The platform was covered in pale cushions and pillows ranging from large to mouse-sized. Sami picked up one of the miniature pillows, and realized it had a sweet vanilla scent. She sniffed, touched her tongue to it; then, suddenly starving, she popped it into her mouth. Its texture was different from any-thing she'd ever tasted—a bit crisp, soft, feathery, and spongy. Its taste was unfamiliar and delightful—spicy and leafy, creamy, fruity, and sweet. "I can eat these!" she cried out, scooping up handfuls of the little pillows, popping them into her mouth. "Oh my gosh. They're so, so good!"

Dorsom sprang to her side, knocking the rest of the little pillows out of her hands. "Sami, those are Shadow food."

"Who cares!" She turned, laughing, grabbing pillows that were spilled across the platform, eating before he could catch her wrists. "These are the best things ever."

Natala put a hand on Dorsom's arm. "She's *hungry*. Actuals can't skim along without food like Flickers can." She ran her silver-ringed fingers over a pillow, and her gemstones' blue lights flashed. "These are vitamins, minerals, and egg. Perhaps they are not so bad."

Dorsom held one pillow up to Bat. "What is such stuff?"

Bat looked wryly at the food, then at Dorsom. "Will-o'-the-wisps, cattails, moonlight," she said in a low voice. "Nutrient."

"Riddles. Evasion," Dorsom muttered.

Bat's queenly face twitched for a moment as she took a step backward.

"Patience, Dorsom," Natala cautioned.

A sly smile spirited over Bat's face. "Flickers always think they can tell what's actual and true, but in reality, they don't listen. They only muddle and eavesdrop on each other's denials and distractions."

"As you like, Shadow creature," Dorsom said impatiently. "Flickers know nothing and see nothing. Just, will you tell us—is this food safe? What happens now she's eaten Shadows' food?"

Bat regarded Sami gravely. "I know not."

"How can you not know?" Natala cried, startling Sami, who was busy dusting off more tiny pillows from the ground—it was the first time she'd heard the serene Flicker raise her voice. "You are one of them! You *have* to know."

Bat glared at her, a cold half smirk on her face. "How am I to know such a thing? Have ever I seen an Actual eat Shadow food before? Has any a one here known such? In fact . . ." She crossed her arms, her manner growing more thoughtful. "To tell the truth, I would have guessed that Shadow food—especially anything found *here*—in the Bare Isles—was too much darkness, too pure for any un-Shadow creature to take in." She lifted her arms, bangles jingling as she dropped them. "I'm curious indeed to see what consequences there are."

Throughout this discussion, Sami had begun to notice the tiny pillows she'd eaten seemed to be expanding in her stomach. Her hunger had vanished and she felt much as she did after one of her grandmother's dinner *hefleh*s, when Teta invited friends and visiting relatives, and they'd spend hours at the table, eating and telling stories. It was a sense of happy contentment along with a deep, bone-washing tiredness. And suddenly Sami felt very tired. Her senses swam around her, blurring colors, smells, and sounds.

"Sami! What's happening?" Dorsom's words seemed to bounce faintly, the group turning toward her in alarm.

"I just . . . need . . . to sleep." She pulled her legs up onto the platform and let herself sink into the cushions. It was an amazing, heavenly sensation, like slowly falling into vanilla pudding. "Just for a bit."

31

A powerful smell was in the air. It smelled a bit like dust. Like wet cement and sawdust and burnt things—*phosphorus*—was that the word for it? Plastic, dust, gunpowder. Like sitting too close to fireworks. Sami opened her eyes to see sharp broken rubble—piles of debris, stacks of cement bits everywhere. Light was coming from a weird place: she looked up and saw the center of the ceiling was crushed. Through an immense hole dangled a tangle of metal rods or pipes. In the back, to one side, was a staircase with a twisted railing of once-elegant metal scrolls that led up to an opening in the crumpled ceiling.

What is this place?

She stood up slowly, running her hands over her arms and face, but she was completely unhurt.

Where am I?

Somehow, this was not a dream. She was very much here, in this place. The light was hot and strong and the air almost wet with humidity—a bit like the air in Florida. Other smells started to emerge from underneath the dust and gunpowder. She smelled diesel and wet pavement, a damp, greasy, roasting smoke. There were also wisps of spices—cumin, cardamom— earthy as the scents coming from an old cupboard.

Sami moved toward a window in the cement wall where street sounds poured in from down below. Just an empty frame; the window held no actual pane—it was like someone had cut the glass out with a knife. Looking out, she could see she was up high, maybe on the top floor of an eight- or ten-story building. Below was a city. Honking cars and sirens filled the air along with children's voices, high and urgent, as they ran through junk piles on the street, tossing a red ball. Men in berets shooed the children, and other men in zip-up white jumpsuits trudged around burnt, splintered wood, metal rods, and hills of refuse as high as snowdrifts. Abandoned shells of cars seemed to drift through the dust. Looking straight down, Sami realized the lower front of the building she was standing in looked like it was completely torn up into a huge heap, like an unmoving avalanche of wreckage between the building and the street.

Studying this view, she thought that something about the scene below seemed awfully familiar.

Her legs turned rubbery. And then her whole body seemed to fill with cold jelly.

Her mother had a few snapshots of herself in her old neighborhood in Beirut, grinning, posing in her navy school uniform, behind her a rubble field and city buildings. Eight or ten stories high.

In one snapshot, Sami remembered seeing a little boy running in the background, almost a blur of movement, holding a red ball.

Now a sound filled the air—haunting and swirling, almost mystical. She knew, without even thinking about it, that this was the *adthan*, the call to prayer. Teta used to say that sound was what she missed the most about living in Lebanon—the daily punctuation, a call to pause and reflect. Five times a day the musical recitation came crackling through loudspeakers on top of the mosques, telling people it was time to stop what they were doing and pray.

At last Sami knew she was in Lebanon. She tried to tell herself she was dreaming. But she couldn't. Somewhere in her dimmest consciousness was the memory of an enormous force hurtling her, smashing her through layers of time and space. Someone or something had gotten hold of her and sent her not into a dream or fantasy, but back into her mother's history.

Sami scanned the room, taking stock of the situation. It looked like this place might once have been some sort of store or workshop. There were wire hangers scattered across the floor, a toppled plastic mannequin, an overturned desk and chair. Near the window stood a large metal frame, which she realized must have held a mirror at one point. Now it was empty, surrounded by tiny glass fragments. The frame itself was silver metal scroll-work in the shape of wild, irregular waves.

The call to prayers stopped and the street noise resumed, although it seemed subdued, as if much of the city were praying silently. She leaned out the window as far as she dared and tried calling out to the people below, but Sami's breath was whipped away in the wind and the distant roar of jackhammers and traffic. The window frame was covered with cement dust and splintered wood. Something cut into her fingers as she held on too tightly.

She leaned back in, turning, looking for a way to get downstairs and out of the crumbling building. Every now and then a vibrating moan and shudder ran through the walls, as if the entire thing was about to collapse on itself. One door led to an empty elevator shaft that descended into piles of trash and broken glass twenty feet down. The staircase stopped after three steps, torn away, dangling metal into the rooms below. But the floors of lower rooms, Sami saw now, leaning over the elevator opening, were blasted out all the way to the ground. The building was an empty shell, barely propped up by a few rusted beams and bolts. She needed to get out of there, she thought, and right away.

She hurried back to the window, and was relieved to see a few men still standing in the street, talking, one of them making notes on a clipboard. She hoisted herself into the wide stone shelf that had once held a glass pane and drew breath deep into her lungs. Cupping the sides of her mouth, she screamed as loud as she was humanly able: "*HELP ME.*"

In the moment of the scream, everything seemed to slow down and magnify: she saw things close up—the silver buttons on the uniforms of the officers, the blade of a toy helicopter trapped in the detritus, the streak of white in a man's black hair. Sami saw the black-haired man shield his eyes and squint up in the direction of her scream. He looked directly at her. And then a thought like a distant whisper reached her through the whirl of noise. *Samara.*

Startled, she froze in place. She seemed to hear her own pulse in her head over all the other noises. Sami and the black-haired stranger stared at each other. Gradually, she noticed there was something vaguely familiar about his face. His hair grew long, then short, and his form changed from male to female and back to male again.

"Do I know you?" she whispered.

I need to talk with you. The thought came to her as if from very far away—farther than the street below—strained and summoned with great difficulty. *I am waiting.*

Who are you? She tried to send her thought back to that distant point. But some force like an onrush of wind swept her back into the room. She hit the floor and felt the impact from her tailbone to the top of her cranium.

Then Sami felt something else, much deeper—another muffled groan, terrible and low, like a sound of dying. It came from all around, from the floor and the walls and what was left of the ceiling above her. The building seemed to shiver, then tremble, and dust and bits of cement and glass started to rain down, mixed up with brilliant sunlight and crazily blue sky. A shard of mirror fell toward her, tumbling slowly, lazily, reflecting the entire broken room, then reflecting Sami herself, stunned. And she knew, even before she started sliding, falling head over heels, that the entire building was going down.

32

A sparkling trail of light cut through the dust. She followed it and felt herself rolling forward, the pressure of a hand on her arm pulling her up out of layers of debris. Her eyelids fluttered, barely opening, and she saw, hazily, shadows of figures. The voice murmured again behind her, and with one big push, she surged forward onto her hands and knees. She started coughing, then her eyes opened fully and she saw the Flickers pull back, startled.

"What's happened to her?" Natala demanded. "What have you done?"

Behind the Flicker, Sami saw a flurry of wings fling open into the shape of a woman. Bat stepped forward, swiping the hair off her forehead with the back of her wrist. A sheen of sweat glowed on her face and her blue tunic was rumpled. "Reach into the time-world is what *I* have done. Where we nearly lost her."

Dorsom held Sami's arm. "I sensed it as well." His voice dwindled and she could see he was examining her face and deliberately not saying . . . something. "I felt something throwing you so far away. I kept trying to pull you out, but you were gone far too far."

Sami coughed and hacked. It felt like her mouth and lungs were full of smoke, like she was covered in it, but after a few moments of swatting at herself she realized there was nothing there. She struggled to sit up, then touched her face and hair gingerly. "What's happened? Have I been here all this time? I don't get this—I know I wasn't dreaming. I was really and truly there—I *know* I was!"

"Certainly, yes," Bat murmured. "You were there. I couldn't see what place it was that was holding you, but I felt it. Only your self-physical remained here—which is the least part of any being."

Natala gestured toward the horizon: a glowing purple-rose sliver of sun was lighting up the trees. "We kept vigil. So worried for you."

Sami hugged her knees, gazing into the distance. "It—it was amazing." She shook her head slowly. "I was in a bombed building—in Lebanon. The Actual Lebanon! And there was someone there—with me."

Who was it? Dorsom crouched closer to her side.

She frowned. "It was hard to see. He was outside—on the street just under me. I shouted and shouted for him, but he didn't hear me. Then I really screamed and I think he saw me—

or maybe he did. But then . . . then—" She slid her hand over her mouth. She looked up at them. "It wasn't really a man. It . . . seemed like a woman—someone a lot like my grandmother. Only it wasn't my grandmother either." She shook her head. "I know it doesn't make any sense, but things just kept—shifting around."

Dorsom and Natala both leaned toward her with questions: *Did you speak? What did she say? How did you get there? Was she the one who brought you there?*

"I can't explain it—not at all. I only know she sent me a thought. She said she needed to talk to me. It was all so much like a dream," Sami admitted, a bit miserably. She rubbed her forehead. "And there's more than that—because it felt like there was something there—in that room—that I was supposed to see." She shrugged and shook her head. "I have no idea what."

The Flickers exchanged glances. Natala nodded at Dorsom. He frowned in thought, then stood and put his hands on his hips. "Sami? There is something, a possibility, we might want to . . . consider. Remember I told you about Reflection? The energy that can pass between an Actual and their Flicker? When a Flicker steps into a mirror, to help their Actual to see better?"

Sami nodded. "I think so. You said maybe you'd show me someday? What it was like, I mean. . . ."

Dorsom lowered his gaze. "Okay, so this isn't exactly the most optimal of circumstances. I mean, of course, the best thing would be for your own Flicker to do this for you. But whoever it might be, that Flicker isn't here. So, if you want, we could try it now. You and I."

Sami frowned, worried by this sudden offer. "Why? What are you thinking that I am going to see?"

"In Dreamtime, you were altered—a bit," Natala said, touching Sami's hair. "It's rather . . . striking."

Sami looked at Bat: she sensed that the Shadow would tell her the truth. But the bat's lustrous eyes gave little away. "Samara—the reality is that none knows quite what this means. But if the Flicker helps Reflect you, you might be able to see something more—to better grasp the meaning of this . . . change."

With a quiet sense of apprehension, Sami agreed to try this process of Reflection. She, Dorsom, Natala, and the Shadow bat walked down the soft slope to the water they called the gazing pool. Hundreds of colors danced across its surface, reflecting the gemstones lining its edges. Sami couldn't really take it in, she was too busy worrying about whatever this "change" was that they'd mentioned.

While she and the others waited on land, Dorsom waded into the water. *Don't worry—I will be with you, just beneath this surface.* He crouched, then sank back into the water so it covered his face and body in a silver sheet.

"I can't see him," Sami said nervously. "He isn't going to stay under there like that, is he?"

Natala studied the sparkling pool. "Our water is full of light and air, Sami. We can stay beneath the surface for hours without needing to come back up."

Bat put her hands on her hips and arched her back, luxuriating in the balmy air. "Gazing pools are especially lovely—they're built for napping. It's the best kind of sleep you can imagine, being rocked by warm, soft currents."

"Here," Natala said. "It works best if you come right down to the edge. Lean out until you see your reflection."

Tentatively, Sami leaned out, watching her watery reflection begin to gradually focus.

Then she stood straight up and with a shriek she clapped both hands over her face.

33

Sami had diamond eyes.

Her round, dark brown eyes had turned into rings of clear brilliance. Even her pupils looked like glinting black gems. And her head seemed to be ringed by a thick great mist, like a halo of smoke. "What—what *is* this?" she gasped, her voice wobbling wildly. "What's happened to me?" Sami stumbled away from the pool, holding her face and blinking between her fingers.

"Now, do not panic." Natala took her arm. "Fine-fine 'tis going to be."

"But my eyes!" She brushed away tears. "And what's all that smoke around my head? Will it change back? I couldn't ever go back home looking like this—my mom would freak!" Sami clutched her mouth. "I can't go to *school* with glowing *eyeballs*! What on earth is this?"

Dorsom climbed out of the water, dripping. "It's Silverworld, Sami." He bent slightly to look into her eyes. "Our physics are different from those of the Actuals. The haze you see here . . ." He gestured around her brow. "This is the Shadow mark that Lamida mentioned."

Sami nodded, remembering. "The sign that they put on me—to help them identify their prey," she said grimly. She tipped her head, trying to get another glimpse of the smoke.

"But the crystalline eyes—this is new to me," Natala said. "Whether sciences or magics, I don't recognize it."

Turning back toward the pool, Sami squinted and widened her eyes—her reflection wasn't as clear now that Dorsom had gotten out of the water. It rippled and bounced light—now her diamond eyes were only swirls and fragments. Sami folded her arms grimly. It was starting to seem like, when literally everything in the world was unbelievable, it was almost easier to believe anything. Then she noticed Bat standing quietly behind the others, staring at the grass as if she were fascinated by something. "Bat," Sami said. "Do you know? What is this? What does it mean when your eyes turn into diamonds?"

Bat kept her face turned away and she spoke as if she were talking to the slim, bending palms. "I remember their songs," she said. "No one should sing so beautifully. It's painful—that much beauty. Even for a bat."

Dorsom studied the Shadow bat. "She's recalling. Remembering something important. Talk to us, Bat. If you care about Sami, tell us what we're seeing."

The woman pushed back her mass of silver-blue hair and glanced at Sami, then at each of the Flickers. "The *Ifrit* of the Mediterranean Sea were known for their gemstone eyes. 'Twas true. I saw them myself—there were as many *Ifrit* upon the waves as there are blinkflies in the SilverNight."

"You believe you saw the *Ifrit?*" Natala breathed.

"Believe and did," said Bat. "Shall I tell you all their names?"

Natala's eyes widened. "Extraordinary. But it is true—some Shadows have been alive nearly since the beginning of Silvertime itself. If she is old enough to have seen the *Ifrit*, then Bat is one of the oldest Shadows alive." She nodded respectfully toward the Shadow.

"The *Ifrit* were hunted-starved to extinction—centuries ago," Dorsom said. "They haven't existed since past remembrance."

"Some Flickers believe the *Ifrit* were only legends," Natala added in a murmur.

"They were no legend," Bat insisted. She lifted her chin and looked at Sami from under lowered eyelids. "Your eyes alone are proof."

"I don't understand," Sami said, but a new feeling, like awareness, rippled down her spine. She touched the outer corners of her eyes.

"It's possible. . . ." Natala nodded slowly. "The Shadow food you ate may have allowed some trait of one of your ancestors to show through."

"You mean—those delicious little pillows? Like, they let my

inner mermaid out?" Sami couldn't help shaking her head as she said it. It was impossible, and yet . . . it echoed so many of Teta's stories. "My grandmother—she always swore we were descended from an *Ifrit*. It was, like, supposedly thousands of years ago. . . . And Teta also had a kind of magical guide—her name was Ashrafieh. But I—I just can't imagine any of it is— I mean, nobody ever really believed that stuff." Again she shook her head in disbelief.

Natala said, "Indeed, there was a famous Flicker called Ashrafieh, famous for her courage and her ability to Reflect."

Dorsom looked into Sami's face. She saw sparkles dancing on the surface of his own eyes. "Then let's try again," he said. "It's time to look within. Let's see what the reflections can tell."

Sami pressed her lips together, trying to resist another swell of tears. "I'm scared. I don't want to look at my weird eyes anymore."

"I will help," Dorsom said. "Rebalancing will help you to become still and to quiet down the fear-voice inside you."

"You needs must look beyond the surface. Quiet yourself within and without, to see what will be," Natala added softly.

Sami looked at each of them in turn. At last her shoulders sank in defeat. "If you say so," she said a bit hopelessly. "But I don't get it."

"Getting it is not necessary." Dorsom smiled. His face and hair were already nearly dry. He looked back at the pool, then at Sami, and offered his hand. "Shall we?"

ЗЧ

This time Sami approached the water with more caution. Dorsom held up one hand as he lay back under the surface, then lowered his arm so once again the water closed over him in a silver curtain.

And again, Natala and Bat stood on either side of Sami as she crouched by the pool. She saw her diamond-eyed reflection and realized with some surprise that the effect was almost pleasing—even if it was startling. She closed her eyes and said to herself, *I'm here to listen. I won't run away.*

She looked at the water but her reflection remained the same. Pushing her hair away from her face, she wondered if she was losing her mind. What did she really think staring at the water was going to tell her? If she were in the Actual World, she'd probably be calling an eye doctor—or a psychologist—instead of squatting by a pool. Overwhelmed by a sense of uselessness, Sami rubbed her eyes, trying to wipe away the tears, but they came too quickly and spilled down her cheeks. She watched them splash into the water in widening circles.

That was when she realized that something was happening to her reflection. Her breath caught in her throat but she tried to stay calm. She would never learn anything, she reminded herself, if she kept running away. The reflection of her hair began to change. It twisted into spirals of copper and cobalt colors, and her diamond eyes tilted like a fox's. Sami's reflected image dissolved and changed into that of a woman.

Now a diamond-eyed creature blinked back at Sami from the water. She looked lovely and yet quite strange, as if there was something wild and animal-like in her face. She shifted to one side and Sami noticed that the creature had a powerful, curving tail covered in scales: it swished through the water, then evaporated into a sparkle.

"*Mermaid?*" Sami breathed.

Once again, the reflection began to alter—the hair swirled, growing shorter with streaks of midnight blue, the skin turned faintly green, and a new woman's face gazed up at Sami. She seemed foreign and yet somehow familiar, as if within the eerie, darkly diamond eyes were glints of Sami—or someone close to her. "You've arrived at last," the reflection said. "We've been waiting."

"You look like the person I saw on the street," Sami

murmured. "In Lebanon. When I was trapped in that crumbling building."

The lime-tinted face said, "It appears that you escaped. That's very good."

Teta's features echoed through the woman's own—the deep set of her eyes, the high cheekbones and delicate lips. "You look—like my relatives," Sami whispered.

A fizzy, burbling energy rippled through the water. "I am *of* your grandmother—we've been joined for a long time, she and I. And you, Samara, are the last of our line. Our last hope for release from the Nixie."

Could this be Ashrafieh herself? Sami felt drawn to the water, wanting to ask—but something made her hesitate. She crouched lower, murmuring, "Are you an *Ifrit*? I thought the Nixie couldn't hurt someone as powerful as an *Ifrit*. I mean—I didn't think *anyone* could."

"All beings, magic or not, have strengths and weakness—as do I, Samara." Spirals of hair floated across the woman's face, but now her hypnotic diamond gaze was intent. "I'm not an *Ifrit*, though one is here with me. At one time, there were so many *Ifrit* they filled Silverworld—they contained both Flicker and Shadow molecules and their energies were limitless. But they were driven into hiding long ago and now they are dying out. Nixie preys only upon weakened creatures she is sure she can defeat." She stopped for a moment and seemed to be frowning into a distance beyond Sami. "So many times I have wanted to dissolve, to escape this prison, but I must do what is necessary, not what is pleasant. . . ."

Her faraway glance reminded Sami of something similar her brother had once said.

They'd only been living in Coconut Shores a few months when Sami came home a little early from school and caught Tony changing into some kind of uniform. "Hey, what're you doing home already?" he'd asked as he clipped on a little black bow tie.

She'd been happy to see him—they hadn't been able to hang out nearly as much as they used to back in New York. "I'm skipping social studies," she said. "That class is pointless. It never gives, like, other sides of the story."

Tony's shoulders drooped and he gave his sister an exasperated look. "You're a *kid*—you don't get to decide what's pointless and what's worth it. It's all *school*. You don't have a choice."

She'd felt something harden in her chest. She almost said, *Who died and made you Dad?* But even in her anger, she knew that was too awful to say. Instead, she asked, "Well, what about you? You have school too. And what're you wearing, anyway?"

He squinted into the little mirror next to his bed. His room in their new house was even smaller than Sami's. "I've got a job, if you have to know. Bussing tables." He wouldn't meet her eyes.

"A job? But you're *fourteen*."

He shrugged. "It's not exactly official."

"What about classes?"

"I have school permission to miss the last two periods. I bike to the restaurant and set up."

Her mouth had fallen open. For a moment she couldn't even

speak. Then she put her hands on her hips. "Was this Aunt Ivory's idea?"

Tony turned away from the mirror. He looked angry—and years older than he was. "It's *my* idea, Sami. Yeah, it's no fun, you're right. But we need the money. Mom's struggling, trying to support us all by herself. And things are expensive down here—especially . . ." His tone softened a little. "Well, I was thinking—if we had a little more coming in, maybe we could afford, like, special care for Teta—here, I mean. At home. Ivory doesn't know anything about this—and neither does Mom. And I don't want them to know about it yet, either." He crouched down and looked right into her face. "Can we please keep this a secret?"

Sami had stared back, not blinking. Everything was on his face—frustration, anger, sadness, but there was also fear. And that made her afraid too. She nodded in silence.

He lowered his eyes. "I'll just try working for a while—until Mom's steadier in her new job and we, you know, we can figure out how to take care of Teta. Don't worry—I'm not going to get to quit school forever. I'll be back at it way too soon." He smiled at her and it was such a sad, fake smile, she couldn't even look at him.

Sami tried to make the woman in the pool stay just a little longer.

"Please wait—where are you right now? How can we help you? Can we come to you?"

But the woman didn't seem to hear Sami. Her sharp, beautiful face rippled, breaking up and re-forming beneath the surface. Sami heard Natala murmuring and a quiet thought reached her: *She hasn't much time.*

"I must speak quickly," the woman was saying. "It was terribly difficult to evade detection—her soldiers are everywhere." Sami saw the woman's eyes glow and her lips part. "Samara, please listen now." Her eyes narrowed, their light was knife-edged. "You must find the Genie's Eye. The most rare. The Eye is a weapon of sorts—a key—and it's the one hope against the Nixie."

The Genie's Eye! Sami leaned closer to the water. She remembered the wild journey she'd made into the sky with the Shadow birds—and the mysterious images she'd seen revealed through the portal—a castle—and an eye. "The Eye—yes. Maybe I've seen something like that. But what is it exactly? Where do I find it?" she pleaded.

The woman's eyes slid away again. It seemed impossible, but at that instant, Sami sensed the woman was afraid—of something or someone. "I shall not survive much longer in this place. And if Nixie is not stopped, neither will Silverworld. The Eye has passed between the Actual World and the *Ifrit* for ages—but it is time for you to return it to its rightful place. Its time is upon us." Through the water, her gaze gleamed darkly—she seemed to be receding, sinking back from the surface. "The Eye must be replaced by the time of the gloaming. After will be too late."

"Wait, please—" Sami begged. "I need to know more about the Eye—and the gloaming! I'm not ready—I need you!"

"The Eye shall be hidden in plain sight!" she cried as the

pool grew brighter, light seeming to crackle and fracture into thousands of flecks. "I give you my blessings and my brightness. Remember who you are: Samara, descended of *Ifrit*, warriors, and Bedouin. Of Flicker and Actual. Brave and strong to the limits, and beyond."

"Oh, please wait," Sami cried as the woman dissolved into blue light. "Wait!" And then, staring into the water, she saw the haze lift from her forehead and the diamond-light in her own reflected eyes fade back to brown.

35

"Guys?" Sami looked from one Flicker to the other. "Exactly when *is* the time of the gloaming?"

No one spoke for a moment. A puddle formed under Dorsom's feet as he dried in the Silverworld sun.

Sami raised her eyebrows. "That soon?"

Look there. Dorsom pointed past the water and the sloping lawn out to the ocean, where Sami noticed a crackling blue haze. It looked almost as if the horizon were catching fire.

What is that? Sami asked, shielding her eyes with her hands.

Natala barely glanced at it. "This is how it happens—just before the beginning. The start of the gloaming equinox," she said. "Once in a Silverworld generation, there's a shift in our lunar cycle. For a brief time there is naturally a greater amount of darkness in the sky than light. On that night, the powers of the Nixie and her Shadow soldiers are at their greatest intensity. They rove over Silverworld, spreading havoc and fear. Clocks go backward, birds tumble from the sky, rain falls upward. Flickers stay in their home-places and don't venture out. During such time, the Nixie is released from her castle. She becomes even more powerful and brutal. She roams and steals Flickers and Shadows alike. None are seen or heard from again."

Sami lowered her face into her hands. *Then this is impossible. We'll never make it in time.*

No. Natala put an arm around her shoulders. "We are beside you. We will help you—no matter what."

"Besides, we've no time to debate this." Dorsom lifted his chin toward the horizon. "The gloaming is not yet here. We'd best keep pushing and save discussion for later."

Sami, Bat, and the Flickers started back on the veering, broken trail. As they walked, the shrubbery seemed to grow denser; flat, eggplant-colored leaves shuffled and hissed, and thick spears of vegetation curled out of the ground like claws. The group grew increasingly quiet, and even though they were trying to move quickly, they seemed to go slower and slower. Sami felt as if the ground itself were clinging to her feet and weighing her down.

After a long, silent hike, Dorsom stopped by a stump ringed with jagged red plants and he passed around a canteen of water. "The air seems hottish and coldish both," he said, rubbing the back of a wrist over his forehead. "How is this possible?"

"The elements are streaked," Natala observed. "And uneven."

Sami puzzled over the intensity of the sky, the way it seemed to grow thicker and murkier even though the sun was still out. And there was a movement in the air, as if something were pushing and pulling back on the light itself.

What do you see, Silverwalker?

She glanced up and noticed Bat watching her closely. Sami held out one hand, as if the light were something she could run her fingers through. *Is this normal?* Sami asked. *It seems to be getting so dark so quickly. And that weird current—like breathing?*

Now the Flickers were listening, the group looking all around.

Shadow soldiers, Dorsom thought-hissed.

I sense them close by. The bat nodded and looked over her shoulder. *The reason we no longer saw the Shadow marks behind us, I think, is because they await us up ahead.*

"A trap 'tis!" Dorsom searched the horizon. "The Shadows snuck ahead of us somehow. Did you know this all along?"

"Never!" Bat's eyes flashed. "I had no idea they'd learned to move so quickly or quietly. I'm just as surprised as you."

"Then truly we *are* trapped," Natala muttered.

A circular breeze stirred Sami's hair around—a bit like her thoughts, turning and winding. It seemed they were blocked, but she refused to give up. At last she said, "Well, I'm supposedly last of the Silverwalkers, aren't I? Doesn't that mean

I have, like, this special ability to move between places? I thought I was supposed to be able to go back and forth and travel around. What if we retrace our steps and go back to the island with the pillow-food? If we all eat it, maybe we could sneak out that way."

Dorsom shook his head, his skin flashing from greenish to silvery-gray. "It's not so simple. The portals are unstable—Nixie's growing power has shaken the structures of the Worlds. It isn't safe to retreat—the Bare Isles themselves are losing their integrity. The colors are off. When the gloaming starts, the beaches will begin dissolving. We can't forward go, nor back."

"It's true," said Natala, pointing to the ground. "Do you feel the vibrations? Subtle they are, but Silverworld grows more and more unbalanced, with seismic and volcanic shifting. The pathways are collapsing."

Sami crouched to touch the earth and she felt it—the softest tingle in her fingertips. She'd been hearing, and mostly ignoring, a low hum at the back of her head—barely more than a whisper—for a while. She hadn't realized all this time that the hum had been coming from under her feet. "Whoa," she said quietly.

"Well, then." Bat put her hands on her hips. "The way forward is hard. Bigger than *each of us*. But the powers of the Flickers can be joined—our energy and concentration can be focused. The path forward is not bigger than us *together*."

Natala put her hand to the base of her throat, her kohl-lined eyes bright and glistening against her purple skin. She seemed to be thinking very hard. "If we converged to join our energies, it would be hard to control. But we might be able to shatter a hole of sorts through Silverworld."

"True. Possibly. Maybe—just enough for Sami to slip through," Dorsom murmured.

"There's grave danger, though. Such convergence could cause fault lines. It might break Silverworld into pieces," Natala said. "It could create enough dust and debris to dim even the Actual World sun." She paused again, as if working something out in her mind. "Yet even so, there *is* also the chance . . . if you were swift, and we focused our intentions—we might create a window, a narrow one, for you to leap to your destination—the Castle Shadow."

Dorsom squinted at the green light. "The gloaming won't be fully on us for a few hours yet. Once it's gloamingtide, though, the Nixie will be let loose. The surge in her powers will be enormous—she will overtake Silverworld, blot out our sun, and certainly begin her attack on the Actual World. She has been building to this point for ages."

Natala shook her head. "This is a decision only Sami can make—we can join our forces, but Sami is the one who will have to jump into a hole in the World." She looked back at Sami. "If we create an opening, we won't know how stable it will be—or exactly where it will send you."

"Or how long last it will," Dorsom added. "Such a hole would try to reweave and reknit itself quickly." He took her shoulders. The softening light shone on his face, and she thought she saw glints of her brother in his dark Mediterranean eyes. He said quietly, "Natala is right. I believe we can get you into a portal, but beyond that, there is no telling."

Sami drew a long and only slightly shaky breath. "If you guys can make this portal, I'm ready to jump into it."

36

The wind was changing colors.

Sami saw shooting streaks of aquamarine, powder blue, and navy as they hurried toward the island beach. Dorsom followed her gaze. "Another sign . . ."

"Don't tell me—" she said. "More about the gloaming."

"There will be changes aplenty," Natala admonished them. "But we must stay sharp on our task. Quickly now! Our powers will be greatest if we join in the surf, let the water unite us."

Sami hung back a moment, foam rushing around her feet. Though they'd crossed between the other Isles without problems, now she hesitated once again at the water's edge, remembering the whirling undersea Shadows when they first crossed the Bare Straits.

"No time to linger!" Natala urged. "This is our single moment."

"But what about all of you?" Sami asked. "What happens after I jump and you're left with a closing portal and an army of Shadows?"

Bat gave her a thin smile. "The Shadows have little interest in us. It's you, Silverwalker, who are the true prize—and the one who must escape."

Dorsom laced his fingers tightly through hers. "Sami, fearless you are. The most courageous and capable of Actuals." His black eyes shone with conviction, though she wanted to ask how many Actuals he knew besides her. Instead, she nodded, took another breath, and together they strode into the rising waves. The water between them and the last remaining island—the one they called Castle Isle—was higher and rougher than that of the earlier crossings. Bat and the Flickers formed a circle of joined hands. Bat was on her left, Natala on her right, and Dorsom was directly across from her. She interlaced her fingers with theirs, squeezing nervously.

"Together we make-shall, together we unbreak-shall," Natala chanted. They repeated after her, lifting their hands up over their heads. She heard the ruffle of Natala's ringlets, saw the tattoos on the backs of her hands flex as the Flicker lifted her arms. Sami began to feel the words on her own lips, reciting with the Flickers as if she'd known them all her life. She knew the words even when they switched into another language that sounded to her a bit like French, a bit like Arabic, and a bit like the older, swishing syllables that rose from the waves. "*Yah, al basah! Ouwai bosa, ouwai besiso!*" Sami kept up, chanting fluidly. The wind grew faster, so strong that it stained the air gray and blue, and Sami didn't know if the agitation in the wind and water was from the gloaming or their spell-chanting or the forces of the Nixie herself.

Gradually, she sensed a trembling that she thought at first was in her legs, then realized was coming from the ocean floor beneath her feet. It rumbled, growing louder. Back on land, a flock of golden-winged falcons burst from the trees and wheeled over their heads and Bat lifted her head to look at them, her face bright. *It is happening*, Sami thought. *It really is happening!* The water began to surge and swell, turning a vivid neon blue, forming a kind of whirlpool at the center of their circle. The water whipped and shoved them, but Sami felt strong, stronger than she ever had before, her legs so rooted, it seemed almost as if, for once, she was the one keeping all the others anchored. Then a kind of well began to form inside the whirlpool, a hole at the center, growing deeper and larger, so they each had to inch back, extending their arms to not lose their grip on each other.

"'Tis the break!" Bat cried.

"The tear in the fabric." Natala's face was stunned yet thrilled. "It's happening. The portal."

Dorsom looked at Sami. Through the whipping water and wind, his thoughts were written on his face: *Wherever you go, Sami, I will be there too.* He squeezed her hand tightly, then let go.

37

Everything went dark.

Sami felt like she was being blasted into a current of air inside a water tunnel. Her hair stood on end and her skin squeezed against her bones. The whirling mouth of the portal sucked her down.

She gasped for breath.

Everything seemed to be getting thinner and longer, including her. The joints and knobs of her vertebrae felt like they were actually starting to separate, her bones seemed to be stretching, and was that her chin at the top of her very long neck? Just when she thought that she couldn't stretch any farther, that the air couldn't get any thinner in her flattened lungs, and that her finger bones were about to pop out of their sockets, she burst out of the other side.

And then she really was flying, skimming through air and

water and blades of grass and dreams. Visions. She smelled the earth, and she was up high, looking down, and she could see small scenes, like fragments of memories inside snow globes. There were two little children—she and Tony—beside a Christmas tree, smashing up wrapping paper into snowballs and pelting each other, the smell of pine and paper twisting together as the two of them laughed wildly.

There was her mother, her hair as shining-black as feathers, with her arms around Sami's scruffy father, ankle-deep in water, smiling and windblown. Then she saw Alia sitting at a wooden table in a library, years before Sami was born, surrounded by fat, hardcover books, studying for the bar exam.

There was the bombed-out room in Lebanon, whistling with wind and shards of broken glass. Then the same room appeared to her again, whole and sun-swept and filled with shoppers, elegant drapes, and porcelain dishes. At a counter, a young woman with a heavy silver necklace inspected a teacup. Outside, there were black-haired children chasing a ball along sidewalks, sounds of people speaking Arabic and French, a bakery with a red canvas awning, a café filled with young people sitting by the brilliant sea. Beirut before the war.

There was a long orange ray that seemed to light up the earth, sand like hammered white gold, a series of low, dark tents that billowed in the wind, herds of goats. Tied in long rows, there were camels and mahogany-dark horses.

There was a group of men crouched in low squats, sipping from tiny cups like the ones Teta had brought years ago from Lebanon. One man stood. He was tall with wary but kind dark eyes. He reminded her of her brother, Tony. A tent flap moved to one side and a young girl with the bearing of a princess came out. She wore a white tunic embroidered with silver and her long, thick twists of hair were braided with silver beads. Perhaps twelve years old, the girl had glowing black eyes and wheat-colored skin. A heavy silver necklace made of coins circled her neck.

She looked directly at Sami and said, "You are made of all your memories, times, and places—those you were present for, as well as the ones that came before, and those yet to come. They are your bones and your power. They bring completion. Balance." The girl held up her hand and Sami noticed she was wearing a sapphire ring on her finger—just like the one Teta had given Sami. "There are three *Ifrit* stones—emerald for the earth and good health, ruby for fire and might, and sapphire for sky and freedom. Only the truly bold in spirit and courageous of heart will know the magic of the Genie's Eye. Complete the trio of gems and there will be freedom."

Sami nodded. In turn, she told the girl, "Don't sleep tonight—the desert raiders will be coming!"

Then she began falling or awakening—the air turned cooler—she felt it in a sudden rush of plummeting. Cooler and cooler. Drier. All at once there was a great bouncing splash of something like raked leaves.

And stillness.

∽∾

She finally dared open her eyes.

There actually *were* leaves—tiny budlike leaves, tender limbs, twigs—some sort of blue shrubbery. The air was the powdery Silverworld air, and the bushes she'd landed in were soft as feathers.

After a moment of letting her breath settle back in her body, Sami set about removing herself from the hedges. She swam around a little before she rolled and tipped out onto her knees in the grass. A sense of anticipation bloomed inside her chest. She was on Castle Isle, she was certain of it. The grass had a sheen and the sky rippled with sheets of crimson and gold light as the sun crept toward the horizon.

Sami got to her feet and scanned her surroundings. Dozens of trees and bushes, arrayed all around, were pruned into fantastic shapes of dancing bears and roaring lions and ships sailing and birds with outstretched wings. Between them, marble walkways with a faint glow twisted through the grass and curved into spirals. There were rows of towering indigo palm trees, their trunks dotted and strung with what looked like necklaces of glittering gems.

She was completely, totally alone.

Off in the distance, at the end of three rows of palm trees, rose the form of a vast palace, its silhouette jagged with turrets and gables, arches and towers. Several gables were topped with flags and banners, starkly white against the glinting silver walls of the castle. They flapped and curled, and Sami felt the same chill that had run through her when she'd first seen the enormous Stone Keeper statue guarding the entrance to the Bare Isles.

"Castle Shadow!" she murmured, then caught herself: the Nixie would be listening. Closing her eyes, she took a deep breath and cleared her mind. Sami imagined a thick cloak tumbling down, covering all of her thoughts.

There was no sign of the Flickers anywhere and she didn't dare risk sending out her thoughts to them. Still, she wished Dorsom and Natala were there as she scanned the fiery, purpling sky.

Sami knew there wasn't much time left before this gloaming happened and the Nixie was released from the castle. She brushed the bits of twigs and leaves from her clothes, smoothed her hair, and pulled her grandmother's ring out of her pocket. She rubbed her thumb over the little gem. Was this ring the Genie's Eye? The stone felt cool to the touch—almost cold, in fact. She slid the ring on and it seemed somehow it had shrunk to fit her finger. And she noticed something curious about its color: something she'd first mistaken for a bit of sparkle was now, quite clearly, a pinprick of light. The stone shone on her hand.

Sami quickly twisted the ring so the gem was cupped in her palm and slipped her hand into her pocket.

Moments later, there was a blur in the sky and she heard the familiar clapping of leathery wings.

38

The flurry snapped into a slot beside her, then Bat appeared, her blue-tinted curls roiling in the wind. "Little good it does to try and sneak around the Castle Shadow," she said. "The Nixie and ten thousand Shadow soldiers have already scented you out."

"*Bat.*" Sami nearly laughed with relief—she had never felt so glad to see anyone. "You found me!"

"The light from your ring. We all saw it. But I was the only one who could reach you quickly. The others will have to struggle and muddle on foot to make their way here."

Sami gazed at the far-off castle smoldering against the red sky. Thick red clouds whirred and spun around its spires and flapping flags. Just the sight of it made her feel cold all over. "It's the gloaming now—it's started, hasn't it? It's under way," she murmured.

"They're here—all around us. The Shadows are waiting." Bat studied the gathering clouds in grim silence. "You mustn't approach the Castle Shadow alone now. Your friends will be here soon enough."

But Sami shook her head and turned, her hand closed around the stone in her ring. Bat plucked up her long skirts and hurried after Sami. "You mustn't! The Nixie! Silverwalker, I beg you."

"No time," Sami said over her shoulder. "She's getting stronger and stronger. It might already be too late."

The rolling turquoise lawn was paved with several twisting routes and one central marble path that led in a straight line to the castle. She considered trying to stay hidden, to creep along the hedges, then rejected the idea. Bat was right—it was too late for sneaking. If Nixie was even half as powerful as everyone said, it was likely she was watching Sami right now. Better to stick to the straight and open path, she thought, and travel as swiftly as she could. Her heart beat against her ribs and when she gazed at the castle, it seemed as if she could actually feel the Nixie there, a presence like hot smoke, waiting silently within her silver walls.

"This is madness! Foolish for both of us!" Bat hissed. "I've come too close already. She'll burn me to cinders, sprinkle me on her wine."

Behind her, Sami heard the snap and flitter that meant her friend had turned back into a bat. "Let me go alone," Sami said without turning. "I never meant to drag you into any of this. Protect yourself now, while you can!"

"If only I could." The bat chittered and circled, then squeaked. "But I shall not let you go alone. I'm afraid I'm with you till the end of it, Silverwalker."

Sami held her head high as Bat circled and wheeled around her. The castle grounds were eerily quiet, filled with amazing topiary. As she passed through the greenery, she thought she noticed whirls and leaping things cut into the lavender-shaded twigs and leaves, shapes that at certain angles appeared to have mouths and eyes and anguished facial expressions. One shrub in particular—man-sized, eggplant-colored—reminded Sami of the Shadow being who'd first defended her to the Rotifer. She stopped and studied the topiary a moment, recalling the way stars had seemed to twinkle in the shadow's body. Bat wheeled over her head and Sami nodded and moved on.

As she walked, she began to pick up on a haze of sounds, voices trickling into her consciousness. It was, she realized, just like the way her mind had been flooded when she'd crossed the Bare Straits, those voices cutting through her with their hundreds of stabbing questions and thoughts. Once again, the murmurs crept into her brain. But this time, she noticed, the messages were different.

They were begging. Weeping. Pleading.

She listened closely, slowing her pace to try to make out the words.

She heard: *I'm trapped. Oh, I'm caught. Oh, help me, please, I beg, help us!*

The pleas rose up, echoing and increasing, more and more cries, filling her thoughts.

Set me free, I beg you! Set me free!

Sami pressed her fingers to her temples: *Too much. Too many voices to hear.*

She was approaching a row of marble columns, glittering and golden, lining the central path beside the palm trees. As she grew closer, she was better able to make out faces caught inside the veined marble pillars. She saw mouths twisted into expressions of dread and horror. *Help us,* they cried. Each column radiated thoughts. *We can't move. Can't breathe.*

Gradually, Sami understood: these were all prisoners—every tree and shrub, every statue and column. Somehow, they'd been cast into and contained inside these altered shapes. Every bit of this lovely landscape, even the manicured lawn, seemed to hold captive prisoners.

Then, at the edges of these pleas, another, darker tide began rolling in—new voices prickled inside her head. These were familiar: the old questions and doubts that had attacked her when she first waded across the Bare Straits:

Who do you think you are?
Why are you doing this?

She stood still, calmly scanning the scene, and felt Bat flutter onto her shoulder, perching there upright like a bird. Sami sensed the creature trying to steady itself, almost as if it were lining its spirit up with Sami's—the way two people learn to move together on a bicycle.

"I'm with you," Bat said. "Don't listen to the others."

You'll never survive this!

The questioning voices grew louder and harsher, crashing into the pleas for help. Sami felt them splashing around her like waves, growing higher and stronger, trying to stop her, to drive her away. But they didn't. To her surprise, she remained calm and quiet inside.

She wasn't afraid.

It was the strangest thing. The voices hissed and charged, yet none of it affected her. All sorts of thoughts spilled in, mixing and circling in different directions.

How dare you?
Turn back.
Help. Help me!

And there was this one that she seemed to hear mingling among the others: *You are made of all your memories, times, and places—those you were present for, as well as the ones that came before, and those yet to come. They are your bones and your power.*

Sami kept her eyes straight ahead and didn't slow her pace. She and Bat soon reached the flight of long, low palace steps, each one perfectly bone white. She climbed slowly, flight after flight, gradually ascending hundreds of steps. These led to a gleaming apron of marble, ringed by seven carved archways. In the center, the largest arch was flanked by statues of extraordinary creatures—rearing pink lions, emerald unicorns, periwinkle gargoyles, dark winged children, as well as other marvelous beings in every color with scales and quills or feathers and horns. Like the creatures in the marble columns, these statues were all twisted into expressions of sorrow and pain. Sami put her hand on one of the winged children and felt a quiver of sadness go straight to her heart.

"'Tis good you have come," Bat murmured. "Brave you are—unlike my Shadowy self. The Bleak Fairy has unbounded powers and mystery, but yours I think may be even greater."

Sami nodded. She felt charged with a kind of building strength and determination. She took another good breath, and as they ascended the last few steps the last bits of doubting, attacking voices faded and wisped away.

The castle's grand double doors towered over them, their dark surface covered with what looked like hundreds of silvery inscriptions in an unknown language. Both of the doors were painted with a huge pea-green eye, so the double door seemed to stare at anyone approaching. There was no knob or latch that Sami could see, so she lifted her fist to give a sharp knock on one of the eyes, when the doors swung open.

Bat's wings made a single startled flap. Before them stood another statue, this one at least thirty feet high and chiseled in the same marble as the smaller entryway statues, so delicately detailed that for a moment, Sami was nearly fooled into thinking it was alive.

It was an exact likeness of the *Ifrit* Sami had seen in the gazing pool, the mermaid she'd spied for a few seconds before it had dissolved away.

The *Ifrit's* twisting hair drifted in white stone around her shoulders, looking as if it had been just touched by a breeze; her eyes were closed and her face filled with powerful love and despair. An enormous tail tapered away from her waist, bent in a U, and rose above her head into a fluke glistening with marble scales.

"It's the *Ifrit*! Why does the Nixie have this statue?" Sami muttered.

"I know not," Bat squeaked. "Nor do I wish to find out."

Sami's hand instinctively tightened around the sapphire ring. She moved closer and studied the creature carefully. One of the stone hands floated high in the air, as if strumming invisible ocean currents, the other was lowered, closed around a dagger. Sami studied its handle, the only bit of color in the marble whiteness: on one side of the hilt was a glittering green stone, on the other was one of deep crimson. Each gem was just about the size of a half-dollar.

She took her hand from her pocket: the ring seemed to hum, as if it had its own tiny spirit.

"The stone, the stone!" Bat creaked. She unfolded her wings and circled Sami, tilting and folding and flapping. "It's singing!"

It *did* seem to be singing, almost trembling, as Sami lifted her fingertips and looked again at the dagger. But there was nowhere to place the sapphire.

At that moment, she heard a familiar voice cry, "Samara, wait!"

Dorsom walked out from behind the statue.

"Oh. Oh my gosh—" Sami lowered her hands and ran to her friend, Bat flapping over her head. "I can't believe it—you've made it. I was so worried. And where's Natala? When did you get here?"

"All shall be explained." Dorsom grabbed her wrist. "But we've got to hurry—the sun sinks—the gloaming will begin!"

They ran out a door in the back of the grand entry and into a vast hallway with polished wooden floors and carved wooden screens. Their footsteps echoed in the corridors as they passed tiled water fountains and birds in immense cages. They raced through an open courtyard, where Flickers in sea-green turbans and robes stood beside rust-colored camels with black eyes.

"Where—where are we going?" Sami gasped.

"We're almost there!" Dorsom ran so quickly, he was pulling her. They passed through another arched doorway and came to an enormous circular gazing pool, the size of a city block. It glimmered sky blue and gold, as if lit by a hundred hidden suns.

"I'll get in and you toss the Eye to me," Dorsom called.

This didn't follow anything the *Ifrit* had said before, but Dorsom seemed so confident, Sami pulled the ring off. Just as she was about to toss it, though, she saw a dark light move over his face.

Something in her drew back. Her fingers closed around the stone.

"Hurry!" he called. "Throw it now."

"Dorsom . . ." Sami frowned, then clutched the ring to her chest. She looked all around but could see no sign of Bat. "I just—just was wondering something."

"What? What do you—?"

"How did you know I was carrying the Genie's Eye?"

He tilted his head, smiling. "Well, Samara, you just said so—didn't you?"

"Dorsom . . ." She crossed her arms. "Do you know—what is my greatest fear?"

His face stiffened with impatience. "We don't have time for games, child. What are you talking about?"

"Just—trust me." She closed her eyes. "I can't do anything until you answer my question. What is my greatest fear?"

He stared at her, then smiled. "Well, of course, your greatest fear is of the dark."

Sami filled with dread. She shook her head. "Who are you?"

"What do you mean? I'm *Dorsom*, of course, silly girl. I'm— I'm your Flicker. Your one and only reflection." He smiled broadly.

Sami turned to run but the doorway seemed to melt into a solid wall. She slapped against it, moving her hands and arms over the solid surface in disbelief. "Let me out!" she cried.

"Give me the Eye," a cold voice said behind her, "you horrid little Actual."

She turned and watched as the fake Dorsom seemed to melt just like the door had. He became a puddle that rose into crackling, staticky gray mist and filled the room. From the mist came a thrumming voice: "Give me the Eye or I'll destroy you and take it."

All Sami's confidence and calm seemed to freeze. Still, she tightened her grip on the ring. "You'll never get it!"

The static sprinkled into the gazing pool and there was a dark flash.

There, filling the huge pool, was an *Ifrit* like the one in the grand entryway. Her gray U-shaped tail flipped and turned, her hair snaked in fat, ashen ringlets, and her eyes were full of crimson sparks. "Give me my Eye," the *Ifrit* said, "and I'll let you go unharmed. Give me what's mine. *I* was the finder of the Eye. It fell from the crown of the old giantesses who once ruled the Worlds. I found it millennia ago, rolling on the ocean floor. You have stolen what's mine."

A voice hissed down from the corner of the vaulted ceiling: "Not *truth*." Bat swooped between Sami and the gazing pool. "Nixie that is—destroyer and deceiver!"

The mermaid roared and rose dripping from the pool, snatching at the bat. The enormous creature kept going, as if she could swim through the air itself, until she floated just above the water—much in the way Sami had seen Rotifer hang above the surging waves. Her hair and arms undulated and her tail snaked back and forth as she looked from Bat to Sami. "You know nothing of who or what I am."

"You're the Shadow Nixie," Sami retorted. "You stole all those creatures and imprisoned them at your palace. *You're* the thief."

"Such a clever one," said the Nixie. "You've become so knowledgeable. Did you know about this, then?" She swept one arm forward and the blue gazing pool vanished, dropping away into an eternal fall.

39

She was pierced by horror. There was something so dreadful about the bottomless opening, Sami felt it was somehow more than total. In the Actual World, even emptiness could have a sort of presence. This was nothing but absence—perfect and limitless. Sami was so terrified by the sight she tried to step away, but her legs turned to jelly and her head swam.

"What is that? What's down there?" Sami managed to ask.

"Nothing is in there," the Nixie hissed. "And everything."

"The void!" Bat shrieked. "Between the Worlds."

"Without depth or death," the Nixie affirmed with her frozen smile. "Things fall without cease."

Again Sami tried to step away from the ledge and once again her rubbery legs failed her.

"Perhaps you would like to give me the Eye now," the Nixie purred. "Or do you need a closer look at the void?"

"Never." Shaking, Sami crossed her arms tightly. "You'll have to take it from me."

"That won't be a problem," the Nixie assured her. "I can crush enemies and traitors with a single blow. Like so." She flicked her index finger and swatted Bat across the room: she struck the wall and fell lifeless to the floor.

"No!" Sami gasped. "Don't hurt her!"

The mer-creature tilted closer to Sami, so her coiling hair spilled forward, and her hands swept over and around, sweeping powerful air currents through the room. "You have so many playmates! I can dispose of you in the same way. Or perhaps you'd rather make some new friends—like Ashrafieh."

"Ashrafieh?" The name echoed through Sami's brain. She was filled with a sense of dread. The Flicker from her grandmother's stories, her guide and protector, was named Ashrafieh.

The Nixie gave a weird hooting laugh that rippled and reverberated through the walls of her palace. "I had to do something to bring you to me, didn't I? I needed you to transport the Eye for me, from World to World. But I also need *you, Samara,*" she added slyly.

"I have nothing to give you," Sami snapped.

"But that's where you're wrong. You are something so special. You were born with the powers of your ancestors—human and Flicker. Finally, after generations of empty waiting, there is one deserving of my Reflecting. I shall become a Flicker again and learn to Reflect *you,* Silverwalker." Her hair twined and twisted as a terrible smile filled her face.

A Flicker? Sami hesitated, but didn't have time to puzzle

over this. She wanted to run away, yet her body wouldn't obey her. And there was something more, something beguiling about the music in the Nixie's voice and her extraordinary laughter that snaked its way into Sami's consciousness. She squatted before the pit, shaking so badly she could hardly breathe. "I would never want *you* as my Flicker," she said, "a monster like you."

"Monster, you say?" Again the Nixie laughed, the sound of it increasingly musical. "The gloaming has begun. Soon you won't be able to resist me at all. And don't forget, Samara—you are part *monster* yourself. The blood of *Ifrit* and Flickers runs through you." Colors of sea green and teal blue rinsed across her face and body and her hair twitched, and Sami watched as the Nixie grew at least another foot taller. "Just give me the Eye," she crooned. "I'll let you go and I'll free your grandmother, too! Oh yes, I know all about her troubles. And I'm the only one with the power to release her. That is why you came to Silverworld in the first place, isn't it, Samara? Just give me the Eye and you can go home a hero."

Horrified, Sami realized she was beginning to feel drawn to the Nixie. Increasingly, everything the Nixie said seemed to ring with truth and music and poetry. The Nixie knew how to free Sami's grandmother—so why not give her the stone? What a tiny price to pay—why, it was almost nothing at all!

There was just a very small, dwindling sense at the back of her mind—the awareness that she'd come for Teta, but that along the journey, her purpose had grown larger and stronger. Sami wasn't here for Teta only, not anymore, but for Dorsom and Natala, for Bat and the creatures imprisoned in the castle and its grounds. For all of lovely, flickering Silverworld. And yet her thoughts were getting cloudy and confused. She knew she'd come to fight the Nixie, but the feeling of it, the necessity, seemed to be moving farther and farther away—as if the monster were lulling her into a trance. The terrible pit that yawned between them might have changed back into a sparkling blue pool again for all Sami knew. None of it mattered any longer— not Silverworld or the Actual World, not the Flickers or her family. It was impossible not to give in.

Sami smiled broadly as the Nixie's laughter rang through the palace, and the walls and floors trembled and rocked as Sami opened her palm and held up the ring. "I'm coming," she said.

The Nixie reached out with her smooth gray hands, leaning so close that Sami could smell salt water and starfish. And at the very last moment, grasping at the last atoms of her resolve—the last remaining shred of her former self—she turned away from the hands and walked into the eternal void.

40

It was like bursting through a sheet of frozen fire.

Falling and screaming, followed by a shriek from the surface. Sami caught a glimpse of ruby eyes, a flickering split tongue, and a taloned, scaly hand shooting out, trying to snatch her back, grazing her hair. She plunged, along with a shower of falling debris, stones, tile, gems, forks, seashells, and what might've been silver backgammon pieces.

Plummeting.

Gasping.

Eyes slit against wind, onrushing emptiness, a distant light above, already fading.

Twisting and spinning, losing all sense of up and down.

She tried to catch another breath, her mind spiraling, dimly aware that she was falling, falling, falling.

It was like all the falls of her life combined and spun in circles—from trees and stairs and the crumbling building in Lebanon. She wailed continuously as the force of the plummet sucked the sound right out of her throat. Seconds burnt into minutes until time itself burnt away, meaningless in the unending dark.

And yet.

Something inside Sami, something larger than she was, started to grow warm. It was a sensation that pressed through her skin and charged her heart and mind, as if she had been waiting for this all along. This thing in her seemed to have no fear of falling—or any other fear. It was a feeling, sensing quality that sharpened her thoughts and gave her presence of mind, even in the free-falling plunge.

Somewhere inside that endless well of falling, Sami perceived a weirdly familiar sensation. Impossibly enough, it seemed she was able to pick up on a vibration that felt like the air in her grandmother's bedroom. "Teta!" she yelped. Teta warbled away in the falling force as if she were shouting underwater. She closed her eyes again, concentrated, and sent her thoughts out in a beam: *Teta, Teta, Teta.*

After a long pause, a thought bounced back: *Here.*

41

The word rang inside her—*Here*—a fiery bell of both thought and voice. Even through the wind, Sami heard it clearly.

"Teta?" she gasped. "Where—are—you?"

"I am Ashrafieh," the sorrowful voice called back.

Ashrafieh. A dozen memories flashed: Sami at three or four, playing patty-cake, her grandmother pointing to her reflection in the mirror: *Who's that in there?*

Ashrafieh.

"There is no 'where' here," the voice went on. "I am nowhere."

"Hear you," Sami gasped as she spun. "Trying to. Hear. I'm—I can't stop."

"You must try to listen, Sami. You must try to stop the free fall."

"How?"

"Samara!" the voice cried, sounding so like her grandmother that even as Sami streaked through the nothing place, she strained toward the voice. Instinctively, her body had started to curl in on itself like a fist. "Call on them. The powers. They will stop you."

Sami couldn't think. She struggled to listen through the rushing winds.

"Free fall is no different from Silverwalking. It's like a mind fall—inside your body and your imagination! If you stop your mind, then your body—it will follow!"

Sami was knotted up tightly, her knees pressed against her forehead, arms wrapped around her shins. She kept her eyes closed and tried to imagine stopping, but she was sick with fear and dizziness. She just seemed to go faster and faster. "It's—not—working," she spat out.

"Don't think of what's outside or around, of edges or surfaces. Turn within. Find your hidden light, your mantle core. Go there! NOW," the voice commanded. Sami inhaled sharply, and like a pulse of pure energy, she felt herself speed to some inside place beyond even blood and bones, a beat of brightness inside pure dark.

Eyes shut tight, Sami looked toward a glowing white light.

She knew she had reached a safe place—far beyond the fall or the void—and she felt it growing stronger, brighter, and larger around her. It was a place she thought she'd visited at least once before, on the day she learned her father had died. In this place were many bits of memories and pieces of thoughts: her parents' voices, her grandmother calling to her, singing an Arabic lullaby, "Yalla Tnam Rima." In this place, she heard other languages and other voices—those of friends and strangers saying her name. She felt them all around her, inside the bright place, stars inside a constellation. She thought, *You are made of all your memories.*

Something amazing began to happen: Sami started to relax. Her hands opened, her knees released, her legs floated out, her arms unfolded. She stopped spinning. Her fall seemed somehow to ease, softening, slowing. She began to feel—almost buoyant. As if she were learning to fly.

She lifted her arms and the wind supported her. She wasn't afraid anymore, but . . . nearly . . . triumphant. She wanted to laugh out loud. And then she did laugh, because she wasn't falling at all. She arched her back and felt herself turn in a little circle. She tilted her arms in one direction, then the other, and her body turned with them. When she flapped her arms, her body rose and she could figure out which way was up. When she lowered her arms, she sank a bit, but could hold herself in place with a single thought: *Stay.*

"Ah. So you are stopped," the voice said. "Good. Very good." Sami heard a hint of surprise. "And you did it so quickly. It took me months of mind fall before I even began the down-slowing."

"You saved me," Sami called softly. "Thank you . . . Ashrafieh."

"You know of me, then," the voice said. Sami could hear her pleasure. "But it was you who saved yourself."

"I remember you talked to me—through the gazing pool?" Sami prompted her.

"That wasn't my physical self you observed," she said, "but that of my mind. Gazing pools can channel mind waves." *And it was a difficult message to send,* she added, switching to thoughts. *Terribly risky to try to sneak thoughts through the water. No knowing when she might be listening. I did it through your friend.*

"Through Dorsom?" Sami asked. "When he got into the gazing pool, he said he was just going to reflect my own thoughts."

He must have been surprised to hear my whispers, she said gently. *He was the true channel through which I spoke. What an extraordinary rebalancer he is. He made it possible for me to break through to you.*

"And now we're together. Here." Sami turned once through the air, trying to make out any shapes or contours around her, but it was impossible to see through the purplish-gray murk—a bit like trying to look past the edges of a dream. "What is this place?"

"The space between the Worlds—the void between Silverworld and the Actual World," the voice said. "In this time of being trapped here, this is all I've come to understand. We're trapped within a kind of portal, in a place that free-falls and keeps falling."

Sami asked, "*How?* How did that *thing* get you?"

She could hear Ashrafieh hesitate, trying to put her answer into words. "There was a time when our Silverskinned went empty—the one shared between your grandmother and me. Our connection is special—stronger than that between most Actuals and Flickers. A most powerful being is your grandmother—she is sensitive and open to the energies of the *Ifrit*. So Nixie is fascinated and compelled by her. When our contact was emptied—even though it was very briefly—I became weakened. It was then Nixie seized and imprisoned me."

It went empty? Sami tried to imagine in what way a mirror could ever be empty. It sounded like something that could only happen here, not in her world. Frustrated, she looked straight up, flapping her arms, craning backward in search of some sign of light. "Well, whatever this place is—it's been real, but I'm ready to get out of here. How about you?"

"For me it's not possible. I fear you needs must leave me."

Sami's head twisted around as she searched the nothingness. "There's no way that I'll do that."

"I've *tried*. For ages. No one escapes the Bleak Fairy's prison. I cannot move or be moved. And you must not stay. The gloaming has set in—I see it in the depth of the grayness. It twitches and deepens. Once it completes, it will swallow Silverworld entirely. Though my powers are nowhere as strong as yours, you must leave now or you'll never have any way to return to your own World. Already I fear it may be too late."

Sami felt her heart tighten, imagining for an instant the colors and creatures of Silverworld lost to the emptiness. Just as quickly, she pressed her eyes shut. *Never.* "Ashrafieh—I know you're not my grandmother. I'm still learning how this Reflecting World works. But I know for a fact that you're a part of her—that Teta isn't Teta without you. She's dying, back in the Actual World, and she needs you. I would never ever leave my grandmother in a place like this and I sure as anything won't leave you, either."

"But the gloaming—"

Sami flapped her arms once with impatience and jumped upward. "Being scared and stuff just holds us back. That's something I learned from Dorsom and Natala. We have to try—there's no other choice. You helped me stop falling—now help me to help you! Guide me to you—send out a sign, any kind of signal."

She could almost feel Ashrafieh shaking her head. "There's no kind of location—there isn't a *here* or place to come to," the Flicker said miserably.

"Yet we can hear each other," Sami insisted. "And not just in our minds, right? Our voices are reaching each other somehow. And I still have a physical body. . . ." Sami ran her hands along her arms. "And you?"

"That I have. Though I'm not sure what is left of me. I've been in stasis—without nourishment or reflection—for a long time."

Sami nodded in the dark. "If you still have a body, then you still can be moved. Couldn't you travel to that same—inside place—that you helped me find?"

"Flickers aren't built like Actuals—you hold your un-breakable energy within yourself. For us, it rests on the outer surface—it is with this energy we reflect. I need color to survive."

Sami crossed her arms, feeling almost comfortable for someone floating in midair. "I'll carry you. . . ."

"No—no—I am quite certain, it won't work—" The voice sounded fainter. "It's too much effort, even to stay here—present with you. . . ."

"Have you ever tried? With an actual *Silverwalker?*" Sami felt bold—it was the first time she'd ever openly called herself that. "Before, when you helped me—you sort of shot your voice, or shouted maybe; it was like I rode on it, on a current."

"I sent you a thought message, but it was you who did all the work of it." Ashrafieh's voice was increasingly distant, as if she were fading away. "I'm slipping. . . ."

"Then let me try now," Sami cried into the grayness, terri-fied of losing their connection. "I'll hang on to you!"

The Flicker didn't respond—she seemed to have entirely gone away. There was no time to wait. Sami wasn't certain of what to do next, but she wrapped her arms around herself, low-ered her head, and tried to go back to that bright core of en-ergy. She reached toward it herself. This time, the way back was stronger and clearer to her. The bright space appeared easily. And there was something more there, another voice or presence she'd felt before, but couldn't quite identify. It wasn't Ashrafieh, she was almost certain. But that extra something or someone was important—she knew it. She reached toward it, listening, thinking, waiting.

Sami, I'm here. With you I am. Do you hear?

Her eyes snapped open and she cried out, "Dorsom!"

42

Sami felt Dorsom's presence as clearly as if he were right next to her, yet she couldn't help saying, "Is it really you?"

For true, it's me. I felt you return back to Silverworld—and I knew when you spilled into the void. I called and called to you, hoping your thought-mind would hear mine.

Sami nodded. "I can hear your thoughts perfectly—I can. Oh, Dorsom!" she cried, full of hope and fear all at once, and she heard her voice tremble. For a moment, she felt wisps of dread creep into her stomach. "It's so horrible here. I can't see or feel a thing. It's like being trapped inside someone's—"

Deadness.

"*Yes.*" She pressed a hand to her chest. "And—and also, there's someone else—Ashrafieh is here as well—with me. She's trapped. We have to help her."

I know.

"You knew?" Sami looked straight overhead, where she imagined the way back would be. "Have you always known she was here?"

We suspected. Ashrafieh has been missing for some time. We didn't know for certain until you joined her.

When Dorsom said *until you joined her*, Sami felt her bright core grow dim and shrink, and her ears pulsed. What sounded like a million other tiny voices seemed to rush in from all directions, all of them throbbing with the same despair, as if she were surrounded by an army of lost souls.

Sami, resist the emptiness, Dorsom instructed. *Pull away from any of the murky places. Now is the time for you to free-fly.*

She nodded firmly, yet couldn't help feeling another shred of worry: *But what if I can't?*

You must, you will, you shall, responded Dorsom.

Must. Sami felt the word echo around her. *Will.* She nodded again, breathing in each resolution. *Shall.*

You needs must travel back to the bright core. You have all the courage you need to take hold.

"Yes," Sami muttered, half to herself. "Yes. That inside place—" She wrapped her hands around her elbows, and smoothed her palms up and down over her arms, calming herself. Contained. Focused. She pushed away stray thoughts or worries—these were meaningless to her now. Instead, there were the voices of the people and creatures she was fighting for, curving around her like a shining banner. She held fast to her determination and felt light begin to grow from within. As it did she seemed to feel some inkling of Ashrafieh as well. *Come to me*, Sami coaxed, calling to the fragile presence. *I'm here, right here.*

As the presence collected, Sami moved toward it, holding out her arms in the way she remembered her mother did while cradling her when Sami was very little. She tried to gather Ashrafieh and with her eyes closed and body lifted, she attempted to move them both in an upward direction, but nothing happened. Her arms moved right through her and the presence dissolved into particles. "Dorsom," she whispered. "What do I do?"

Her loss and grief are overwhelming her, Dorsom thought-murmured. *Is there some way you can become like your grandmother for a time?*

Under different circumstances, Sami would've laughed out loud. She wasn't some kind of expert rebalancer Flicker like he was. She and Teta were totally different! Her grandmother was a Bedouin warrior who knew about spells and fairies and led caravans across the desert and raised a daughter in Beirut and moved across the world.

And Sami, well, she was still just learning about herself.

How was she supposed to *become like her grandmother*?

There had to be a way. Sami trembled with effort, trying to bring every aspect of her grandmother into her mind—her long braided hair, her black eyes, her tales of the jinn and the long night marches under the brilliant moonlight.

Then an idea came to her.

43

Sami began to sing.

It was an old lullaby. She hadn't ever tried to sing it herself. It was something she'd listened to all those nights when her mother had to work late at her office and her grandmother sang her to sleep. She realized she knew all the words, the sweet, lilting melody naturally rising and falling from her lips, making her brightness glow and seeming to soften the darkness all around.

Yalla tnam Rima . . .

She felt the shreds of Ashrafieh's presence return.

Yalla tnam Rima, yalla yijeeha elnoum.

Slowly they gathered, intensifying, taking on physical form as a diffuse light grew around them. She began to make out the Flicker's form and features. "You've come back. I can almost see you!" Sami cried.

"I dreamed that I'd died and gone. Perhaps I did," Ashrafieh said. "Then I seemed to hear the voice of my Actual, dear Serafina, drawing me back and back. And it was you."

"Just me," Sami admitted.

"And so glad am I that you've summoned me back."

Black eyes stared up at her: there was the familiar soft nose, the wide, gentle mouth, the heart-shaped face. This was what Teta had looked like years ago, before everything started to go wrong. The two wrapped their arms around each other and Sami felt Ashrafieh's sadness start to lighten in Sami's arms. They rose very slightly in the air. Excited, Sami began to sing more confidently and the grayness around them receded some more.

Yalla, yalla . . .

They crept upward. "Do you feel that?" Sami cried out, midsong.

"It's working," the Flicker agreed with a smile. "We rise."

Up they went—inch by inch. Once again, Sami started to feel the swirl of touches she'd first sensed under the water when they crossed the Bare Straits. But this time, instead of challenging her, the brushing wisps seemed to murmur, *Take me.*

Please, me.

Take me as well.

They sprinkled along Sami's feet and ankles, weightless yet present. "Hello, creatures; hello, my Shadow friends and captives," Ashrafieh said.

"They tickle!" Sami said. "I never knew Shadows could tickle."

"I am learning many new things as well," Ashrafieh said, her head barely higher than Sami's chest.

"You are?" Sami couldn't believe anything as wise as a Flicker still had things to learn.

The Flicker pulled back from their embrace without letting go. "I never knew about your Actual heat and sounds—the warmth of Actual blood, and your heart music. I always was curious. And silverous splendid it is!" She laughed, then looked startled. "Goodness me—it's been ages and ages since I heard the sound of my own laughing."

They began to rise faster and faster; when Ashrafieh laughed they shot several feet straight up. Sami craned her head back, scanning for some sign of the surface, when she heard Dorsom's thoughts again: *Sami, I feel you growing nearer now. You must gain more speed as you go.*

"We're going as fast as we can," she assured him.

Faster still. His voice was intent and urgent.

But Ashrafieh shook her head, saying, "I understand his thoughts." Sami felt them slow a bit. "He means we must gain speed to break free. With the gloaming, the darkness grows denser and thicker. It will settle over everything. I forgot about that; the choking thickness will come. I didn't remember. I wanted freedom more than I wanted to think." Ashrafieh sighed. They slowed even more.

Sami wrapped her arms even tighter around Ashrafieh. "Please don't lose heart. Not now! We're really moving. I can get us both out of here—I *know* I can. But I need you to help me."

Ashrafieh shook her head, trembling, eyes closed. "It's not possible. Not workable. It was my mistake to feel hope."

They slowed to a stop, then sagged a bit as the Flicker grew translucent in Sami's arms. Desperate, Sami looked back up and felt her heart swell. It was very faint, almost invisible, but there was one tiny speck of light, less than a pinprick, far over their heads.

I'm waiting for you, Dorsom thought. *The surface is so near now!*

At the sound of his thoughts, a surge of hope jolted through Sami. Suddenly radiance surrounded them in the pit. Ashrafieh squinted and twisted her head away. "By Rotifer! Your *eyes.*"

Sami blinked slowly, seeing shadows sweep through the brightness, then retreat. The *Ifrit* light must have returned to her eyes, turning on like a photosensitive battery. Everywhere she looked was lit up with two tunnels of light, bright as day. She had to take care not to look too directly at Ashrafieh, whose eyes were no longer used to seeing light. Instead, she turned her gaze upward and the beams created a glittering pathway straight over their heads.

"Balanced and beauteous!" Ashrafieh cried, shielding her eyes. "I see it—the starry night."

Sami kept her mind focused only on escape. She didn't worry about the Nixie, the gloaming, or the Shadow soldiers. She and Ashrafieh were still deep in the void—her illuminated vision made that much clear. Sami noticed then a sparkling mist collecting around them. Glitter formed, circling their feet, as if the emptiness were full of crystals. She swished one leg through the air and her motion left a sparkling trail.

"The creatures!" Ashrafieh said. "They're joining their light to ours. Their energies."

"But I thought they were Shadows." Sami gasped. "No color energy or anything."

The Flicker looked at Sami with a twinkling solemnity. "Even Shadows contain a form of color as real and lovely as that of Flickers. Shadows were my companions in the abyss—they helped me keep my sanity with their whispers and poetry." She gazed around at the gathering stardust. "I had no idea there were quite so many."

"It's like a sea," Sami marveled. It felt as if piles of tiny golden sands were rolling up under her feet, gently nudging them on. They began to move upward again, their energies united.

44

At times they seemed to move at a crawl, other times even slower, but eventually Sami noticed the speck of light overhead start to grow in size. Details began to emerge from the night: she made out knobs and roots gnarled into the sides of the pit. She saw slashes and claw marks and splatters.

Dorsom. Sami sent out a quiet thought. *Are you there? Where is the Nixie?*

I'm here with Natala, Dorsom responded.

Hello, Sami, Natala joined in. *I am sending you both strengthening energies.*

We entered through the western archways of the castle, Dorsom thought, *but have yet to see Nixie. All the castle doors are flung wide—we fear she may have started her escape into Silverworld.*

Sami and Ashrafieh both felt the murk begin to accumulate once again, growing heavier as they neared the opening. It felt like a kind of thickness, as if the air were turning into cream or custard, then mud or plaster. The light beams from her eyes grew fainter and Ashrafieh clutched Sami tightly. "Whatever happens," she muttered, "thank you, Silverwalker, for believing—for both of us."

"Thank you," Sami said, "for not giving up."

Now you must both fight, Dorsom thought. *I am here. I join my light to yours. To you I give my full power as a rebalancer.*

As do I as well. My full power as rebalancer, Natala added.

The Silverwalker and the Flicker took deep breaths and Sami instinctively lifted her arms like a swimmer, stroking through the murkiness. It felt increasingly dense, as heavy as wet sand. She sensed that if she let herself think about it, she wouldn't be able to breathe. So she didn't think, she just kept punching her arms through the murk, pulling herself and Ashrafieh upward with her thoughts, her energy, her arms, and the force of the beings around and under her. Somewhere, dimly, as if he were being pushed back by the layers of night, Dorsom thought-called, *Pull, Sami . . . pull. . . . Harder . . .*

She was getting tired, her mind and body exhausted by the effort. The Shadow creatures churned under her feet and Ashrafieh thought, *Freedom, freedom.* But Sami's arms began to weaken and her neck and shoulders ached. The air was too heavy: it felt as if a sludge had begun pressing inside her—into her mouth, nostrils, and eyes. After what seemed to be hours of straining, Sami barely had any strength left. Each stroke she believed would be her last. Then she took another one. She couldn't bear the thought of failing her grandmother, Ashrafieh, and all the Shadow captives. She couldn't stand imagining Silverworld swallowed by the Nixie's eternal emptiness. Yet the task began to seem—as Ashrafieh had said—nearly impossible.

Drowning, suffocating, crushing.

Dorsom's thought cut through the murk, a distant beacon: *Sami, you can.* Giving it every last bit of effort, Sami thrust her arms forward, thinking, *OUT, OUT.*

And her right hand sliced cleanly into open air.

45

It was like bursting through a skin.

She and the Flicker went flying, trailing corkscrewing currents of brilliance and stars, of Shadows filled with sparks and will-o'-the-wisps of light and uncountable other beings, all of them shrieking and squealing and spilling free.

Sami landed, thumping and rolling across the cool tiled floor. She leapt up, scanning and blinking. The room was illuminated with stripes and banners of light, like an aquarium crammed with deep-sea fish. All around her, Sami heard the liberated creatures crying out in joyful voices and thoughts: *Free, free, WE ARE FREE.*

Then both Dorsom and Natala were there, flinging their arms around her. "You did it," Dorsom whispered intensely, over and over. "Entirely, you did it."

Oh, Sami, you're alive, Natala thought. *Really and truly alive.*

Sami wrapped her arms around both of them at once, hugging them fiercely. *We all are.*

Dorsom grinned. "You pierced through the gloaming, Sami. Don't you realize? Nothing like that has ever been done before."

"You saved Ashrafieh," Natala added. "And you broke through the gray matrix, exploding its skin. Now the Nixie no longer has any power to hold or confine. The Shadow spells are broken."

Sami lifted her head toward the top of the castle, blinking at all the colorful beings and in-between wisps twirling sparkling trails of joy. She laughed, waving at the creatures who sent out showers of brilliance.

Natala helped Ashrafieh to her feet, then bowed before the Flicker and touched the back of Ashrafieh's hand to her forehead. Dorsom turned and did the same.

"Most Venerable Flicker," Dorsom said. "We are most honored."

"Daughter of Worlds Beyond Worlds," Natala said. "Hybridity Most Exalted."

Renowned is Ashrafieh through all the Silverworld—a master Reflector of many generations, with royal bloodlines to the Ifrit, Dorsom thought to Sami.

Sami watched as the older woman's hair grew lush and long, her eyes began to shine, jingling silver hoops appeared on her ears, a heavy silver necklace circled her throat, and ribbons of Bedouin tattoos emerged, twining around her wrists and hands. This was the Teta of fifty or more years ago, fresh from the desert, a scent of jasmine, sand, and lemons still on her skin. Ashrafieh glowed faintly sea green and her hair glinted blue, but she looked like one of the old black-and-white photographs of Teta restored to vivid, powerful life. In Ashrafieh, Sami now saw an essence of that wind and sand that Teta must have missed when she moved away from the desert. These things were always a part of Teta, but they'd faded from her life in the city.

Ashrafieh laughed, a girlish, tinkling sound, and waved away their admiration. "Here is the one to be honoring." She kissed Sami's cheeks, three times on each side, then placed an arm around her shoulders. "After being imprisoned—" Her voice rose sharply, as if about to crack. She took a breath, went on. "For years imprisoned, in a void of despair, lost to the Worlds, I was hope-drained, washed bare. Then this child—this *Silverwalker*—came to do exactly what I'd secretly believed was impossible. Now, I and multitudes of Silver Beings are freed."

Behind the group of friends, the thick, old gloaming layers of the void began cracking apart, breaking up into rubbery spurts of dust and ash. Sami turned in time to see darkness surge up from the opening, then collapse back in a hissing rain. At the same time, a noise began growing from outside the castle walls. It sounded like a gathering crowd: there were voices and shouts. Natala looked out through one of the high arched windows and gestured to the others. "Come look!"

The soft Silverworld night was lit up with pinwheels of

colors, shooting sparks, and squiggles of brightness. Standing by an open archway, Sami felt tiny airborne Flicker and Shadow creatures, newly released, their colored trails shimmering over her, circling her wrists, ankles, and waist, each of them like a burst of sweetness.

"They are thanking you," Ashrafieh said. "All those many who were once imprisoned, now freed."

Across the lawns, mauve hedges trembled and opened into shrubbery that glistened with flowers like tiny cups and bells. "The vapor plants bloom," Natala breathed. "There is a language tree!" She pointed to an immense gold-trunked tree, its branches unfolding like the spines of an umbrella. The night itself seemed to glisten more brightly through the open windows and archways, the air fresher, and filled with life.

"The Great Balance is restored," Dorsom said, stepping back to take in the sweeping view.

We shall open all the cages and boxes, Ashrafieh added, spreading her arms wide. *The Castle Shadow is filled with them. We shall burst all the strongholds. Every Shadow and light being must live free.*

The topiaries lining the courtyard began to dissolve or burst into showers of brilliance, releasing all sorts of creatures— lions, elephants, a great beaked griffin, each shaking out their limbs, stretching, squawking, or roaring. Row after row of columns started to dissolve as well—a deep groan emerged from all around the castle and trembled in the walls.

"No need to open cages," Natala said, looking around. "The confinements are exploding open like the void itself."

"I think it's time to make haste," Dorsom said, pointing out cracks racing across the ceiling.

Ashrafieh agreed. "Half this palace was constructed of imprisoned Flickers and Shadows. Soon there will be pillars and windows and railings falling everywhere."

Sami and the others had to thread their way back through the palace rooms to the grand entrance, as none of the windows or doors opened to anything but more enclosed courtyards. Sami wished there were time to linger over some of the marvelous things she saw piled in the halls—mosaics, fountains, libraries filled with fluorescent books and paintings that seemed to shiver as they passed. But more than that, she wished she knew where Bat had gone. Picking up on her worry, Dorsom tried to reassure her: *A Shadow bat as wise and old as she would surely evade the Nixie.*

Sami wasn't so sure. She remembered the vicious way the Nixie had swung and swiped at the tiny bat. But there wasn't time to discuss their next move: pieces of tile kept smashing from the ceilings in spouts of dust and stones. Open cracks sped through the walls. They had to keep moving, faster and faster. Suddenly, a tremendous groan issued from the ground and the marble floor seized up, shattering, and thrusting out enormous jagged shards. Soon they were no longer walking swiftly, but running with all their might.

46

The group approached the corridor to the grand entrance, but as they hurried Sami began to notice something odd: it seemed to be growing darker within the castle, the atmosphere humid and heavy.

Picking up the specific density of the shadows. Natala's thoughts streamed back as they ran. Her hand was lifted, her rings flashing deep blue and topaz. *It's odd. Its matrix thickens. Much like that of—*

The gloaming, Ashrafieh finished.

No analysis or fears now, Flickers, Dorsom put in. *Focus on the castle doors.*

By the time they got near the entry, the air was thick as custard and so murky they couldn't find the grand entrance.

What is this? Sami wondered, slowing and turning in place

beside the others. The Flickers moved their hands through the air, marveling at the gloom.

Ashrafieh moved closer and silently took Sami's arm.

Natala punctuated the silence with a single thought: *Look.* She was staring straight up.

It was almost impossible to make out anything in the murkiness, but something was moving on the ceiling, dense and shapeless. Two great red eyes near the center glared down at them, and Sami heard it thinking: *You broke my prison!*

It massed like a thunderhead, growing and crackling along the ceiling, filling the high, vaulted spaces.

"Whoa." Sami craned back to look. Ashrafieh squeezed Sami's arm.

Dorsom took her other hand. *Hold still,* he thought quietly to the group. *All hold.*

For a moment there was no movement, then a loud, red crackle burst from the cloud. A pure white bolt hissed over their heads. The group gasped and for an instant the entire room was lit up. Sami realized the arched doors to the outside world had once again disappeared.

No, no. The thunderhead rumbled with laughter. *You won't be slithering free this time. The Shadow palace is sealed. I shall take my time deciding how I will dispose of each of you.*

Another bolt sliced through the air, and Natala cried out. The air smelled singed and hot.

Ashrafieh's grip tightened, but Sami pulled away from the Flickers, calling out to the dark creature, "I'm the one you want—aren't I? Let the others go."

"*Yes,*" the Nixie screeched, just as Sami heard *No* flash through the Flickers' minds. Then a tiny snippet of light caught her eye. It spun like a pinwheel near a corner of the ceiling and she heard a familiar chittering and flapping. "Bat," she breathed.

The Nixie grew thicker and ever more condensed, grumbling angrily. A bolt shot through the room and Sami saw everyone's face frozen in place, staring up at the beastly Shadow. The creature mounded high, about to strike again, when Sami noticed another thread of light spiral into the dark, followed by another and another. It was the will-o'-the-wisp creatures Sami had drawn out of the Nixie's pit. Bat was leading them as they bounced and coiled and bounded into the room, igniting the space with sparks and tinselly light. They followed the Shadow bat in brilliant scrolls around the Nixie and filled the space with sparks and gouges of light. Infuriated, the Nixie bellowed wildly, shaking the walls and slashing bolts through the air again and again.

Sami backed against the wall, the lightning strikes so close, she could smell a dusty char in the air. She tried to search the room with each flash, but they came and went too quickly. Her knees trembled and for a second she felt too frightened to move.

Sami, Dorsom called to her. *Remember the pit. How you clawed your way free.*

She nodded. She was still that person. She was a Silver-Walker. The faces of her family returned to her—her wise father and strong mother, there was Tony, laughing and running on the sand, the beautiful beach, and Teta, smiling, telling her:

It is within you, everything you need. Then she was seeing the faces of her new Silverworld family as well—Dorsom, Natala, Bat, and Ashrafieh. Both families joined in her, in two sets of memories yet the same self.

Then she heard Rotifer, its deep current of a voice tolling, saying again: *A double-being shall emerge, a child of Actual Nature and Flicker-lit, a child that shall Cross and See, a child named of soil and sand. That is the one who Stands Between and Restores.*

She closed her eyes against the scorching Shadow flashes and felt herself growing inside her skin. Strength and breath rushed like new blood through her body; she grew more alive and more powerful than ever.

True Silverwalker, Samara Washington, the question is, do you accept your powers—and your fate?

Her eyes flew open.

Nixie. Sami stepped in front of the Flickers. *Enough.*

47

*S*ilverwalker! the Nixie shrieked. *I shall smash you from the Worlds.*

The floor itself seemed to tilt and shift but Sami never stumbled. Reaching into her right pocket, her fingers ran over the cool surface of the stone. As the long icy strands of the Shadow Nixie began to curve around her legs, Sami closed her eyes, touching the bright place inside herself, and slipped the ring onto her finger. It fit perfectly.

"NO," the Nixie roared, releasing Sami. Frenzied, it clawed at the air. "Remove it. Remove the stone!"

Now a tremendous white, opaline bolt cracked through the room, lashing the stone hilt of the mermaid's dagger.

The enormous sculpture began to shake seismically, shattering sheets of concrete, marble exploding like panes of glass. The air filled with dust; rocks rained against the walls and burst the windows. A sound like the earth itself was turning and groaning rose into a bellow, wild, infuriated, mad, and terrifying.

Sami and the Flickers ducked just as some vast green gleam swooped overhead. For a moment, all she could see was the flaming green light, green scales, a wilderness of tangling blue and sea-green color, like living water rapids, which Sami finally understood was hair. She looked up, the room illuminated by the wash of green and blue and silver. She saw two powerful arms, a mouth like a red gash; a being rising thirty feet tall, the top of its great head nearly brushing the vaulted ceiling, its grand shoulders and torso wrapped in golden silks, its hips tapering into a glowing fish tail that slammed and pounded the floor, rocking the foundations of the castle. The great thing twisted, screeched and wailed horrifically, writhing as if it believed it was tangled in nets, its eyes shut tight.

Ashrafieh seized Sami's arm, squeezing. *She's entranced. Her mind is ensnared in a state of capture.*

Another deep tremor like that of an earthquake ran the length of the castle, sending vibrations up the walls and across the floor. Now Sami felt more than power; she felt rage. She was enraged for the mermaid imprisoned in stone, for the creatures large and small who had been tormented by this horrid being, and she saw all of this imprisonment in her own grandmother, broken and failing, and bound to her own form of prison in the Actual World.

Sami turned back to the Nixie and watched it seething and

bubbling like a burned syrup, covering the ceiling and back walls. *It is over*, Sami thought to the creature.

You are over, the thing hissed, and sent out bolt after bolt of hot white lightning.

In the past, Sami might have cowered or hid in fear, but now she walked closer, the sapphire stone burning on her finger. With each step, she felt herself growing in height and dimension. The ring began to hum, the vibrations once again singing in a high, singular voice. Removing it, Sami discovered the stone turned in its setting. Moving it carefully with her fingertips, Sami found the back of the gemstone that had faced the inside of the setting was cut and colored with the image of a wide blue eye. She rolled it until a round pupil and blue iris stared directly out of its gold setting. The Genie's Eye.

It shone, a golden beam cutting through the Nixie's murk. In response, the Nixie deepened; it spat out flames and seething bolts. They lashed Sami's body yet no longer held any heat or substance. She closed her fingers around the ring and felt the Nixie's frozen misery and hatred encircling her skin, then shattering into fragments. The creature's madness, greed, and fury scattered like drops of mercury.

You're reflecting the Nixie! Dorsom thought-cried.

Rebalancing her! Natala joined in.

The Nixie intensified its electrical strikes, throwing out stronger and louder bolts, its center even denser, but along its edges, the immense cloud trail was growing translucent and pale. "No," the Nixie roared in an ice-cold voice, thundering against the walls. "You will never destroy me."

A shuddering moan rose up from the mermaid. Sami whirled around and without thinking tossed her ring to the creature. Though the *Ifrit's* eyes were still shut tight, she caught the ring, then popped it into her mouth and swallowed.

The mermaid awoke. She sucked in a whooshing breath and opened her eyes: one was diamond bright, the other was sky blue. The Nixie's thunderhead contracted and balled against the ceiling, a tight, curdled cloud, crackling with sparks of lightning, shrieking. Sami walked right up to it, batting at it with her hands—it was nothing more than smoke and noise. She waved her fingers through its substance, fanning it away.

Mine. It was not so much a word as an instinct that rumbled from the mermaid. Sami nodded and stepped aside. Now the mermaid swept a webbed hand through the air, snatching the cloud—tiny gusts of shadow puffing out between her fingers.

"RELEASE ME," the Nixie shrieked. "*RELEEEEASE.*"

Instead, the mermaid opened her crimson mouth so Sami spied a row of pearlescent, pointed blue-white teeth, and poured the Nixie down her throat.

And for a moment after that, there was nothing but silence.

48

"**S**he . . . *ate it.*" Ashrafieh gasped. "The *Ifrit*—she . . . incorporated . . . the Nixie."

"Marvelous marvels," Dorsom said, his eyes round. Then, after a stunned moment, he threw his arms around Sami and Ashrafieh both. "Nixie is *done.* Do you understand? *Silverworld* herself is free."

Natala ran to them, laughing. "Freed we are! The old proportions will be restored. We shall be Flicker and Shadow in balance—in the way it's meant to be. And no more dread of the Nixie and her soldiers."

Ashrafieh squeezed Sami so tightly the breath left her chest. *You did this, Silverwalker. The Remaking of Worlds.*

"Me? Ha!" Sami shook her head. "It was *all* of us. And . . ." She straightened and approached the mermaid. The entity towered over her, bigger than two Rotifers. "You did it as well," she said directly to the mermaid.

The grand creature smiled, her diamond eyes burning ever more brightly. Sami trembled to stand alone like this in her presence.

A soft, creamy light laced with baby blues and lavenders was starting to glow in the room, lighting up its corners and edges. In the distance, they could see a sliver of the crowning Silverworld sun. The mermaid lowered her face till Sami was looking into two brilliant irises. Gently, the being reached over and stroked her hair with one webbed index finger, as if Sami were a pet sparrow. *Brightness comes,* the mermaid thought-hummed. *Like dawn.*

The mermaid's thought-voice was deep and bell-like, tolling in Sami's mind so richly that it seemed to echo. But her language, if you could call it that, was hard for Sami to grasp and difficult for the mermaid to translate—set more into feelings than words. Ashrafieh stood beside the enormous one and interpreted for her, thinking: *After years of entombment in these walls, she says she will once again swim the airs and breathe the waters.*

The *Ifrit's* grand tail swept powerfully over the floor, the flukes flexing and stretching. The Flickers gathered around her, respectfully quiet and slightly awestruck.

"How did it ever happen?" Sami asked Ashrafieh. "I mean, how did the Nixie ever capture *her?*"

Evidently the mermaid understood, because her laughter

was tremendous, sounding through the corridors like a whale's song.

Ashrafieh smiled sadly: *Eons ago, the Nixie and mermaid were friends—but that was in the days when all beings were Ifrit—changeable, magical, and fluid. When the Worlds split apart, dividing up creatures and kingdoms, Nixie's mind altered. She grew too dark. The mermaid was her first victim. While she slept on her rocks, Nixie cast a spell and seized her in molten rock. She would never die, Nixie said, not realizing—or caring—that she would stop living as well.*

"Nixie's victims lived in similar sorts of captivity," Ashrafieh added softly. "Your teta as well."

"What?" Sami craned to face the mermaid, her heart turning over in her chest. "What about Teta?"

Shall we tell her? Ashrafieh looked up, and the mermaid nodded. The Flicker lowered her lilac eyelids and clasped her hands loosely. "For more than a year—an Actual year—your teta has garbled both her words and thoughts." She looked again at the mermaid. "She did it deliberately. To protect us. So the Nixie couldn't know what we'd planned."

The mermaid swept one sea-green arm through the air, indicating all the creatures that Teta had protected.

So Teta *had* been doing it on purpose, Sami realized. Then something else occurred to her—it was just a year ago that Sami's mother sold the house and the family moved to Florida. Sami remembered her old mirror had been packed and sealed inside a moving box—and her grandmother started fretting and pacing, repeatedly asking why they couldn't just carry it by hand, like the old movers had.

Ashrafieh nodded. "Serafina and I were uniquely connected through the mirror. Nixie feared your grandmother might be a Silverwalker and wanted desperately to destroy anything that might pose a threat to her power. When the mirror was covered, it weakened our connection—just for a short while—but it gave the Nixie an opportunity to seize me. She brought me here and threw me into the void."

The mermaid rumbled something, and Ashrafieh translated: *Through the void, our minds traveled to each other like sea vines. Our bodies were captive, but our minds roamed silently, carefully—always carefully—to evade her detection.*

"We could risk only a rare few words, every few days, to make our plans," Ashrafieh added aloud.

Dorsom's face was furrowed with thought. "Ashrafieh—was it *you* who brought Sami to Silverworld? Not Nixie?"

"I didn't have the ability to bring her through the Silverskinned myself." The Flicker's round, eggplant-dark eyes lit up. "But I knew who did. I sent Sami dreams about her grandmother's spell book. And the mermaid whispered to Nixie of the Genie's Eye, which she coveted for its pure energies. She believed that anyone who owned it possessed the ability to control both Worlds. Together, the mermaid and I fed Nixie enough bits of insight to grasp who the *real* Silverwalker was. It was a grave risk, but it had to be done."

"So Nixie was the one who opened the mirror, but it was

your idea that she do it," Sami marveled. "And Teta? She knew your plan, but couldn't risk talking about it at all."

"She hid both her thoughts and words," Ashrafieh confirmed. *Shadows can move into any corner and listen through any Silverskinned. If Nixie had sniffed even a hint of our plan—if she'd had even the slightest sense—all would've been destroyed.*

Those scrambled words and that silence and strangeness— Teta had done it to save her friends, Sami thought. She felt grief for her grandmother's pain but also deep pride at her loyalty.

And even through all that, your connection with your teta was close enough that you still understood each other, Ashrafieh said gently.

Until she wasn't strong enough even for you to follow her thoughts, Dorsom added. *Her signal grew too weak.*

Once again, sounds of singing and celebration reached them from beyond the castle walls, and brilliant lilac- and rose-filtered lights began to fill the room. Dorsom put an arm around Sami's shoulder. "Day breaks. The gloaming is coming to an end. We'd best leave the castle while it still stands."

The mermaid nodded, but Sami saw a trace of melancholy in her smile. *Once upon a day the Nixie was my truest heart,* Ashrafieh translated for the great creature. *I'm sorry I had to envelop her.*

49

Outside, the periwinkle lawns glistened in the rising sunlight as all shapes and sizes of Flickers and Shadows sprang in and out of the bushes, breaking free of columns and sculptures, jumping out of the paintings, tile work, and carpets. The castle itself began to dissolve away down to the simplest framework, as almost all had been constructed—walls, gardens, art, and windows—of stolen and enchanted creatures. A white tiger soared over the grass while a griffin shrieked and stretched its pink wings.

Using her powerful tail, the mermaid bashed down three of the remaining castle walls to free herself, as it seemed the entryway had been constructed around her. They crumpled easily as the vaulted ceiling dissolved away into clouds. Working together, Sami and the Flickers and dozens of Shadow and light beings all helped to carry the mermaid outside, and place her on the lawn beside a sky-blue fountain.

"You have the weight of an Actual being!" Dorsom laughed, shaking out his arms.

"She has the weight of the Nixie inside her now," Natala said. "That of a thousand stolen souls."

The mermaid closed her eyes. She stretched and arched on the velvety grass, drinking in the Silverworld sunlight.

Admiring her glowing form, Sami asked, "How will we get her all the way to the beach? It'll take days for us to carry her, at this rate."

Ashrafieh tapped the tiled side of the fountain. One of the few remaining castle structures, it was big and round as a gazing pool, bordered by a low wall covered in blue-and-white mosaic tiles. "All waterways on the Bare Isles lead to Mother Ocean."

"The fountains are spring-fed!" Natala exclaimed.

"How brilliant," Dorsom said. "And great good fortune for us. No more carrying!"

There was a rattling sound in the bushes and a small pink light being—a sort of cat-dog—came through the shrubbery holding something gently in its jaws.

"Ah." Dorsom crouched and put a hand on the being's neck, removing the object from its mouth. "There she is. . . ."

"Oh. Oh my," Natala said softly.

It was a lifeless amber-colored bat. "No! It can't be." Sami gulped, crouching. "Oh, Bat!" She picked its limp form up carefully. "Maybe she's just knocked out? She survived the first time the Nixie struck her down. Maybe she's still . . ."

But Dorsom was shaking his head. "She darted straight into Nixie's face, when we were embattled—to distract and turn her eyes."

"She was Shadow-burnt," Natala said regretfully, then murmured, "bold, brave thing."

Brave, thought Dorsom. *Through and through and through.*

Sami flashed on a memory of light whisking and chittering as the Nixie raged full of lightning. Her vision softened with tears. "She was my guide—more than once. She was there when I arrived on Castle Isle, the last steps of the way. She showed me—" Her voice broke off as she dashed away tears with her knuckles.

The mermaid's big hand closed around the bat, and the small, fox-faced animal transformed into its broken human form, her glowing hair spilling over the mermaid's arm, pale blue lids shut over her eyes, a single white bolt like a slash of paint crossing her hair, face, and chest.

For a moment there was only the distant sound of Flicker and Shadow creatures celebrating and cheering on the lawns. Then Ashrafieh nodded at the mermaid and thought, *In the Actual World, she would be gone and done. But the mermaid believes some shreds of her Shadow hover here still. I feel some force yet as well—though it too has gone very far and will soon be done.*

The mermaid turned her diamond eyes to Sami with a bit of caution and delicacy as Ashrafieh explained: *She proposes to take her to the Old Kingdom—to see if they would call her back.*

"She would do such a thing?" Dorsom asked reverently. "That's no small matter, the act she speaks of."

The mermaid touched the tip of a finger to Sami's face and her tears turned to a sort of powder that drifted away. Ashrafieh translated for the mermaid: *I owe the Silverwalker a life and such gratitude.*

Sami's eyes filled again, though this time with joy. "Oh, if you thought you could save her! I can't even tell you—"

She can't save her in the manner you're thinking of, Samara, Ashrafieh cautioned.

"Bat is gone from our Worlds forever," Dorsom said. "But in the Old Kingdom, her spirit might live on, playing and singing and adventuring, with others gone away. She would know and remember us, and even sometimes she might send us messages from the Kingdom."

Natala touched Sami's arm. "And there are yet other obstacles—for you, Sami. When this gloaming is over, the last of the portals will be destroyed—the Nixie's work is coming all undone."

"It's true—the paths between Worlds are dissolved," Ashrafieh agreed. "It is the work of years to rebuild them."

"While I would rather keep Sami with us," Dorsom said, "isn't it true that the ways between the Worlds become one within the ocean? That in the greatest depths, there is another portal, far away, in the mermaid singing fields?"

"They were the gatekeepers to the hidden Silverskinned—a mirror they called the Glass Water," Natala added.

Sami remembered Teta telling her of the "silvery mirrors" of desert oases and mirages of water and secret doorways that travelers would stumble after for miles in the hot sand, never reaching them. All reflections—Teta had said—of the same one true doorway, buried somewhere in the sea—the water that all the deserts and desert dwellers remembered and longed for.

The mermaid nodded. She lifted a finger to Sami's brow, and Sami felt something fizzing lightly around her head and chest. She looked up, startled and delighted. New energy spiraled up from the soles of her feet, winding around her legs and arms and expanding her ribs. Her bones strengthened; she felt clearer and lighter, as if she'd grown feathers—or gills. "Wow," she murmured. "What *was* that? I really—I feel different."

The mermaid flexed her tail, one strong arm slung over the edge of the fountain.

Ashrafieh stroked Sami's arm. *No time for unbelief. The Ifrit must return to water, so you'd best say goodbye to your friends now.*

Sami blinked. "Right this minute? We're going now?"

Come with her now or nevermore, granddaughter, Ashrafieh said. *And she shall lead you home.*

50

There was a sweet, sad look in Dorsom's eyes—as if he felt he was about to lose his best friend. Sami knew it was time, this was the return home that she had longed for, and yet now she didn't want to do it. She looked to Natala and Ashrafieh, each of them gazing at her with the same mix of love and sadness. "I mean—I know—I'll come back to visit for sure," she blurted, giving Ashrafieh, then Natala, a tight hug.

Sami couldn't look at Dorsom when he approached with his arms out. She stared at her feet through a glaze of tears. "I don't know how to say goodbye to you," she said in a tiny voice.

"No such of a thing as goodbye in Silverworld," Dorsom said. "We say: *I you shall see again.*"

Sami slowly lifted her eyes to his and saw them fill with indigo light. She said, her voice breaking, "I you shall see again," then hugged him.

He squeezed her tightly, and she felt something seem to glow between their chests, as if their heartbeats were echoing each other.

Just look in the mirror, Dorsom thought, using the Actual World word, *mirror,* his forehead pressed to hers, *and I shall be there.*

I will look for you, Sami thought, *always.*

They released each other, then studied each other's faces for a long moment, and Sami was once again startled by the sensation of looking at her reflection.

Ashrafieh's thoughts broke into her own: *Samara, it is time.*

Sami nodded and put her hand in the mermaid's much larger one. "Goodbye, beautiful Silverworld," she said, then stopped. "I you shall see again," she corrected herself. "All of you."

Dorsom only smiled and nodded. "I you shall see again. And again. And again . . ."

With that, Sami followed the mermaid, who had eased herself into the grand fountain. There was a stone pillar at its center, which, Sami remembered, had once held a sorrowful cherub spouting water. When she slung her feet in, she was startled by the cold and depth of the water—it went nearly to her chest. She gulped air, expecting to feel the familiar old panic seize her. But nothing happened. The mermaid smiled and nodded, then, with Bat in one hand, she seized Sami with the other. Sami felt a quick downward tug, and Silverworld turned into a rainbow of color dancing on the watery surface over her head.

Breathe!

The mermaid's thought was gentle, almost silky, as they

glided through the water. Sami's vision was nearly as clear as it was on land, and she realized the mermaid seemed transformed, her body glittering with blue luminescence, her hair bright. Yet, oddly, she also appeared somehow more human—smaller, softer, even motherly. She swam a spiral around Sami, sending circles of brilliance through the water as she did.

Breathe.

Sami blinked. There was no way she'd thought-heard the mermaid correctly. *Breathe?*

The mermaid turned and slowly nodded. She was telling Sami to breathe.

I can't breathe water, Sami protested. *I'll drown!*

But the mermaid closed her eyes and shook her head. *You won't.*

Even though she marveled at her new ability to swim with such grace, she couldn't imagine trying to inhale. Her chest was locked in place, her throat closed off, as the mermaid swept her hands over her own throat.

Breathe, breathe.

After a few more moments of swimming, the need for air began to press; her lungs ached. Sami took one last glance at the surface, the glowing sea fans and winking scarlet fish—if she was about to die, she supposed, this was the loveliest place she could imagine doing it. Her lips trembled, and her chest burned.

Then she noticed something like a dance of color in the water. She looked up into a pink tangle of leaves or vines or . . . tentacles.

Rotifer?

A lilt sped through the water like an ocean current. They were swimming inside the clear mantle of the Rotifer.

All will be well. The great creature's thought shivered through her mind.

Sami was filled with a sense of reassurance and well-being. Her chest relaxed, and crisp Silverworld water entered her nose and throat. And, again, nothing happened.

She took another, larger breath—water rushed in, expanding like air, and she realized it was true: she could breathe the Silverworld ocean. It was thicker than air, but she quickly adjusted. Her lungs filled and emptied, and she felt strong and fearless—as if inhaled seawater were just the nutrient she'd always needed.

Sami let go of the mermaid's hand, put her own palms together, then pushed them apart, shooting through crystalline seaweeds and lilac urchins. The mermaid smiled at her across schools of celadon fish. *So this is what it means to swim,* Sami thought, stroking, then twining and twisting through the water. *I love it.*

51

They swam side by side, Sami and the mermaid, protected by the Rotifer cape. In the crook of the *Ifrit's* arm, Bat's blue hair spiraled in the water. They passed through plains of sea fans, reefs, corals, and starfish, through plant life that grew up from the ocean floor as thick as forests, past schools of laughing dolphins and staring pink hammerheads, around the rainbow spines of lionfish, around bioluminescent deep-sea creatures, and under the marigold belly of a whale. At some point in their journey, long after Sami lost track of time, she realized they were slowing down.

Finally, the mermaid pointed beyond the transparent mantle, through strands of seaweed. Squinting, Sami saw what looked like a deeper, round section of water: it glittered, and she couldn't see anything within.

The portal. Sami hesitated, then swam to Bat's side. She seemed to be sleeping, her hair swirling all around her limbs. *What will happen to her?*

The mermaid gazed silently at the drifting form.

I hope she'll return, Sami thought, touching the bat's hair. *She was the truest friend.*

The mermaid lifted her diamond eyes to Sami.

And me? Sami couldn't help wondering. *What will happen to me?*

The *Ifrit* carefully placed her hand on the top of Sami's cranium, and again she felt spangling brightness run through her, powdery sparks flying from her fingertips. It felt like a gift, though one without a name or meaning.

Silverwalker. The Rotifer's voice rippled down from above, surrounding. *Nixie is destroyed, your destiny fulfilled. If ever you should need of us, imagine my name and I shall respond.*

Glistening colors spilled down over Sami's head and arms. Her heart filled with courage and her breath deepened. It was time to go.

The mermaid and Sami slipped out from under the lip of Rotifer's mantle. Sami swam backward a moment, waving up at the great creature as three of its tentacles fanned through the water. *Farewell and good health, brave Silverwalker! I thou shall see again.*

She returned to the mermaid's side. Before them, the portal swirled and pulsed, red, then clear, like a whirlpool in the ocean's floor.

Sami hesitated before it. Tentatively, she reached toward the unlit opening. It felt wetter and heavier than the surrounding water, yet somehow familiar; there was a scent of something sweet and earthly. Suddenly she had a memory of lying on warm sand, counting clouds alongside her brother, a soft wind billowing over their heads. She felt a piercing longing for the clear skies and water of Coconut Shores.

She turned to the mermaid and bowed. *Goodbye. Goodbye, Silverworld.* The mermaid smiled fiercely, showing her bluish-white teeth, her spiraling locks and silk wrappers, and sent her arms out wide. Then Sami was being swept off her feet, the portal drinking her in one gulp. As she was tossed through a cascade of bubbles and froth, Flicker voices rang back to her: *I you shall see again.*

52

Collapsed, not breathing. Wet and not wet. Lying on her side, turning. The sun bright and hot.

Air, heavy and fragrant, rushed into her lungs, and Sami's chest expanded. She gasped and coughed, twisted onto her hands and knees, sputtering water, head lowered. Very gradually, she caught her breath, slowly realizing she could breathe normally again.

Sami rolled back to sitting. Pulling wet hair out of her face, she looked around. She was on a gentle slope of wet sand, waves rolling and breaking just a few feet away. *Home.* She stood cautiously and felt the mixture of Silverworld and Actual World waters evaporating from her clothes and skin.

The sky was a cloudless sapphire, and white birds arced over the ocean. Shielding her eyes, Sami admired the way the sand itself seemed to mirror the sunshine. She was standing on a short stretch of beach just a few blocks from their house. The sand felt warm and soft, with the familiar substance of the Actual World. It was good to stretch her sore muscles, to feel the humid air. The early-morning sun felt like a kiss on her head.

She realized, as she walked, that she was happy. Her chest rose with gratitude, and she inhaled the scent of gardenias. How she'd missed her home! Home was the place where her family was, but it was also *this* place: it had grown roots inside her—almost without her noticing. Florida had become a part of her and she was a part of it.

Tony was sitting on the couch as she walked in. He wore his usual shorts and T-shirt, but there was a blanket crumpled around and under him and his hair stuck straight up.

"Well, hello." She laughed, hands on her hips. "I guess you slept there all night?"

"Sami!" He jumped up and swooped his arms around her. "Oh, Sami, oh thank God."

Sami laughed with surprise, but hugged her brother back. "You missed me? For real?"

"What the heck? Where *were* you last night? What *happened* to you?" He took hold of her arms. "Wait a second. Man, look at you—it's like you grew overnight."

"Ha, good imagination," she said with a smile, and headed for the stairs. "Is Mom in her office?"

"Wait—where are you going?"

Sami started up the stairs. "I need to talk to Mom—and Teta, too."

"Sami, they're not here." Tony stood at the base of the stairs.

Something in his voice made her stop. She turned and looked at her brother before taking two steps down. "What do you mean?"

He shook his head and Sami realized he was having trouble answering. Her pulse begin to throb in her throat. "Is Teta okay? What's wrong, Tony?"

He shook his head again and finally said, "She's—she had a pretty bad night. Almost like she was having trouble breathing. She was tossing in bed and sort of moaning. I'd swear I heard her say something about falling—twice. It was the first thing she's said in, like, forever that I've been able to understand."

"She said she was falling?" A shiver ran down Sami's spine. She felt the deep plunge into the Nixie's void again.

"I'm not exactly sure—but it was scary. Lots of groaning and twisting around in bed. I guess she's feeling better now."

Sami frowned. "You guess? Tony, please, where is Teta?"

He lowered his eyes. "Mom took her—pretty early this morning. It was still dark out. To that place. That home?" He lifted his eyes. "I guess she didn't want to upset us—they kind of snuck out. She doesn't know you weren't in your room last night. I covered for you—said you were doing homework," he added in a low voice. "Mom texted a little while ago and said they thought it would be easier on everyone if they just got Teta settled in first and then we could go visit."

"What's the name of the place again?" She was already at the front door.

"Hold up! Where are you going?" Tony scuffed on his flip-flops.

"To get Teta!"

He followed her out the front door. "There's nothing we can do, you know. They don't want us hanging around right now."

Sami turned to him. "Do you know the way? To the nursing home place?"

He lifted his arms and let them flop against his sides. "Yeah, it's off Breezeway Ave. But what are you doing? How are we supposed to get over there?"

Sami looked at him like he was a little slow. "We've got bikes, remember?"

Tony followed her into the garage. "It's all the way across town!"

"So? It's a small enough town." Sami climbed on her bike, threw her lock into her basket, and took off. "Keep up!" she shouted over one shoulder.

She flew over curbs, over the cracked sidewalks of their neighborhood, and under the wide, flat canopies of the poinciana trees. Pretty soon she could hear the whir of Tony's bike just behind her. "How are you biking like this?" he panted.

Sami squinted through the sunlight and wind as they moved into the bicycle lane and sailed under the long, narrow shadows of palm trees and condos. It occurred to her as she pedaled that not so very long ago, she probably wouldn't have done such a thing—just hopped on her bike and ridden. She might've waited for a city bus to take her, but she never would have weaved and dodged, circled around car doors and little dogs on leashes and old men curved over their walkers. Now she almost felt sorry for her old self—how timid she used to be and how much she missed out on because of it. As she pumped, her senses raced, spotting each obstacle, darting to the fastest path. Sami took her bike over an especially high curb and sliced through a puddle, throwing spray. She called back to Tony, "Watch out for that one."

When she didn't hear an answer, she twisted on her seat and realized her brother was about eight blocks behind her, puffing as he pedaled and shouted directions.

We're coming, Teta! She tried to push her thoughts through the air, as she had in Silverworld. *Hang on.*

She zigzagged across a great gray sea of parking lots, up to the automatic glass doors, then jumped down and rolled her bike into the bright lobby. A flowing sign hanging over the front desk said SILVER BEACHES MANOR. A woman in a teal nurse's uniform scowled at Sami's bike and sent her to the rack outside the lobby. Tony was just coasting into the lot as she locked up.

"Where did you learn to ride like that?" he panted. His face shone with sweat.

"C'mon, we can talk later." She held the door open.

In the waiting area, the receptionist lifted a narrow black

eyebrow when neither Sami nor Tony had any identification. She tapped and tapped, searching for Serafina Alattar, then finally pointed at her screen. "They're just moving her in now. But I can't admit kids without a guardian or some kind of ID."

Sami pleaded, "I just got back from a long trip, and I'm super worried about her. My grandmother hasn't been feeling well, and I know it would make a huge, huge difference to her if she could just see her grandkids."

The receptionist looked sternly at Tony, who half nodded and mumbled, "Um, yeah. Yeah, that's totally right."

"Grandkids?" Again, she lifted one pointed eyebrow, then sighed. "Let me call the room." Holding the phone propped between her ear and shoulder, the woman clicked long, crimson-painted nails on the counter. She tapped her pencil several times more, then put the phone down. "No one's picking up. She's probably not done checking in. Why don't you go home and wait there? I'm sure your mom will be able to bring you by later."

"No!" Sami shouted, then she felt Tony's hand on her shoulder. "I—I mean, I'm sorry. But we just bicycled here from our house. It's all the way on the other side of town. It took us, like, forty minutes. Almost an hour. We're *so* tired and we had to dodge all this traffic! Besides, we're just super anxious to see our grandma—it would mean so much to us." Sami made her eyes as wide as she could.

The woman's deep green gaze met Sami's for a moment before lowering. Sami noticed a little silver mermaid pinned to the lapel of the woman's blazer. "Oh, I love your pin," Sami blurted. "Mermaids are so cool!"

"Oh yes," the woman said with a tiny smile, then frowned, suspicious. On an impulse, Sami tried sending a thought to the woman: *Please, please—you've got to help us.*

Something seemed to flicker across the receptionist's face: she blinked. Then shook her head and said, "Well, I must be out of my mind. Come on, while there's no one around. I guess it can't hurt to just go take a peek."

They walked through a window-lined atrium crowded with jungle-green ferns and waxy flowers. By a potted palm, a woman with flyaway white hair patted a curved leaf as if it were a friend's hand. The other end of the atrium opened to a long corridor of rooms. A few doors creaked as they walked by and some residents peered out, their lined faces studying Sami and Tony. At the end of the hallway, there was a small heap of suitcases and books. The receptionist stopped, tugged her blazer down, and knocked on the open door. "Hi, hi, anyone home?" she sang. "We've got a little surprise for you."

The room had a set of French doors that looked out over a garden and the walls were painted a soft watery blue. Sami's mother was hanging up dresses from an open suitcase and Ivory was either trying to hand a teacup to Teta or take it away. Sami's grandmother was sitting hunched, nearly swallowed up by an oversized armchair in the corner. Her eyes looked enormous in her shrunken face and the knuckles stood out in her fingers as she gripped the armrests. When Sami and Tony walked in, she stared at them blankly, mute and frightened. Sami could see her grandmother had absolutely no idea who they were.

53

"Teta!" Sami ran to her grandmother, threw her arms around her, and gave her three fluttering kisses on each cheek—just the way Teta had taught her to do when Sami was a little girl. It was their special kiss. But now Teta just seemed to be confused by it.

"Sami—Tony! How on earth did you two get here?" Her mother held a dress and hanger in each hand. Her eyes looked red.

"Yes, and what exactly do you think you're *doing* here?" Ivory put a fist on one hip. "We're trying to get your grandmother settled in—with as little upset and disruption as possible."

"You mean you wanted to sneak her in here," Sami responded coolly.

"Ah, I'll be going now." The receptionist ducked her head and backed out quickly, pulling the door shut.

"Samara!" her mother snapped. "Apologize to your aunt this instant."

"All right, fine. I'm sorry, Aunt Ivory," she recited. "I shouldn't have been rude. But, Mom, please—please—just wait a minute. You don't know the whole story." She swiveled back to her grandmother. "It's okay now, Teta—you can talk again! It's safe to come out. I know what you did—how you were scrambling up your words, trying to protect Ashrafieh. But you don't have to do it any longer—Silverworld is safe. The Nixie, she's gone for good." Sami was about to say *a mermaid ate her*, but she glanced up and noticed Ivory, her mother, and Tony gaping at her.

"Sami, please," her mother said in a too gentle voice. "This isn't the time for Teta's fairy stories. You've got to accept the facts. Your grandmother isn't well. In fact, she hasn't spoken at all since last night—" Alia broke off, her voice cracking slightly, and Sami realized with a shock that her cool, strong mother was on the verge of tears. "This isn't easy for *any* of us, believe me. But we've decided to go with this facility because—well, I'm afraid for her! And I think they'll give her the sort of care she really needs."

Sami ignored the fearful dropping sensation she felt in her stomach. Instead, she turned briskly toward her grandmother. "Teta, do you hear what my mom is saying? She doesn't think you should be at home—with *us*. Don't you have anything to say to that?"

Her grandmother's face was a complete blank. Sami wanted to shake her, stamp her feet, shout *WAKE UP* as loud as she could. But she realized nothing like that would really work. Fighting off her own tears, Sami remembered how, when something was difficult, Dorsom told her to make her mind quiet. She closed her eyes and squeezed Teta's hands as she thought as hard as she could: *Please, please come back. I know you're in there.*

Sami opened her eyes. There was a long, awful moment of silence. Alia sighed. Finally, Teta's lips parted, but she produced only a tiny, grating sound, as if her voice no longer worked at all. Sami's heart dipped. She heard Ivory saying quietly, "We really should finish moving her in now. She's probably pretty tired out."

"No, you're right," Alia said. "It was a long morning."

"Everything look okay in here?" An orderly in a white jumpsuit appeared in the door, startling Sami. He had warm brown eyes and a kind smile. Sami noticed his nameplate said DORSEY. "Can I help with anything?"

"Oh, we're fine—just sorting some things out—" Ivory started to send him away.

"*Merci . . . Dorsey*," a voice interrupted from behind Sami. The sound was small and hesitant, yet quite clear. "But that . . . won't be necessary."

A hesitant smile broke across Sami's face as she turned around. Teta was sitting straight up with her arms crossed over her plump chest, her chin raised. The bells of her sleeves fell back, revealing the rows of faded, lacy tribal tattoos along the backs of her arms and circling her fingers. "Almost . . . two years . . . without putting . . . two words together. You'd think . . . I'd get a few seconds . . . to start speaking again."

"Mother?" Alia's eyes were wide and her lip trembled. "*Ummi?*"

Teta smiled wryly. "Yes . . . daughter. I'm right here."

Alia said something in Arabic that Teta answered in Arabic, and Sami realized she'd somehow understood.

Alia had said, *This must be a dream.*

Teta had answered, *Not at all, my daughter. . . . You're wide awake.*

Then she held open her arms and Alia lowered herself into them with a sob. "I don't understand," she cried. "How is this possible?"

Teta faced Sami, her eyes wet. "It was my granddaughter over there. . . . She understood . . . that . . . I was in prison. She kept trying . . . struggling . . . until she freed me."

Shaking her head, Alia held both her mother's hands in her own. "But we saw doctors, speech therapists, psychologists! Dozens of tests and assessments. No one knew what was wrong with you. You mean to tell me that *Sami* could figure out something that none of the experts could?"

"Experts!" Teta tossed her head. She seemed to be growing stronger by the moment. "None of them . . . cared about me . . . the way Sami did. None of them had the key. . . . But Sami worked on it. She wouldn't give up . . . even when everyone else said I'd never learn to speak again." She gave Ivory a significant look, and Sami's aunt turned away, scowling, her face reddening. "The only reason . . . I'm here talking my foolish head off right now . . . is because my granddaughter freed me."

"But—but—*what key?*" Alia's face swung from Sami to Teta and back again. "I don't understand. What did you *do?*"

Sami opened her palms as if to show she didn't hold any magic tricks. "We worked on it together, me and Teta, step by step. At first, I thought Teta was sick or something was, like, broken in her body. But then I realized she was fine—that it was more, like, a decision she made, in her head. She didn't think it was safe to talk—not out loud, not even in her thoughts."

"A . . . decision?" Alia looked so baffled, Sami decided to take a different approach.

She laced her fingers together, saying, "Maybe, even, it was sort of like the way I felt about moving to Florida? Okay, I know that sounds weird, but wait. It was like, I used to tell myself there wasn't anything good here—that I could never love it like New York or feel like it was *home* home, or whatever. I didn't mean to, but I couldn't help it. I needed time to find out that it really was okay here too. Like, sort of to *let* myself be happy here? So, it's like once Teta felt like everything was safe, I knew she would start talking again."

Ivory stared at Sami, incredulous. "You mean—all that time—your grandmother could have spoken?"

Teta cut in with her delicate smile. "Physically, yes. But it wasn't a choice—there were people I had to protect. I couldn't even think about them."

"People? In Lebanon, you mean? Memories from the war?" Alia asked softly.

"In both worlds," Teta said, and raised her eyebrows at Sami.

"So you pushed them away. Suppressed everything . . ." Alia shook her head. "I've heard of people doing that. I mean, after Joe died, I couldn't even—" Her voice trembled. Sami held her breath, gazing at her mother—it was the first time in ages she'd heard her say Sami's father's name. "Oh, I just miss him, that's all." Alia smiled then and pushed a stray hair behind Sami's ear. "Still, it's amazing. Really, for you to be speaking again? To reverse all of that silence, after so long? I can hardly believe any of it."

Sami knew her mother's powerful litigator's mind was at work—smart and skeptical, filled with questions and interrogations. In the long run, Sami knew, Alia wouldn't be satisfied with this answer. She would have to tell her the whole truth someday. And she did want to explain Silverworld to her mother, she realized, but not just yet.

Still, at that moment, all her mistrust seemed to subside. Alia laughed and hugged her daughter. "Oh, who cares! Your teta is talking again. It's a true miracle is what it is. Explain it to me or don't explain it to me. I don't think I'll ever understand what happened in a million years."

The orderly in the doorway cleared his throat discreetly and said, "So, will you all be needing help packing everything back up again?"

Sami smiled at him and nodded. "Teta is coming home."

54

That night, as she changed into her pajamas, Sami glanced at the mirror at the foot of her bed, its silver frame like the curling white waves on the ocean. Tonight, the glass was calm and silent—nothing called to her from within its center, and Sami wondered if anything ever would again. She tossed her clothes into the hamper with a sigh, catching a last faint whiff of the airy Silverworld ocean on her T-shirt. *Good night, Dorsom,* she thought, looking again at the silvery mirror.

A few minutes earlier, she'd said good night to both her mother and grandmother, who were sitting together in the living room, laughing and sighing, catching up with each other, talking like two people who'd been separated for a couple of years. Which, Sami supposed, they kind of were.

Now she could just make out their voices through her

bedroom wall. Her bedsheets were cool and delicious as she stretched out, enjoying how good it felt to be home again. Really and truly home. Though she already missed her Flicker friends. She thought about Bat and Natala and Ashrafieh, their dear faces reemerging in her imagination. Then she let herself think about Dorsom. She missed him in the way she missed a best friend, wishing he were right there, the two of them laughing and whispering about their adventures, and she wondered if there wasn't some way to bring Dorsom back to the Actual World for a visit. Sami closed her eyes, and images rushed back to her of waving to Rotifer, of flying and breathing in the Silverworld Sea, of falling into the void and slowly rising out. She recalled a moment in the grayness when her grandmother's Flicker told her, *Never be anything less than you are.*

"Sometimes I'm not sure who I am," Sami had said.

Ashrafieh had gazed into Sami's face as they floated together in that endless void, before they began their escape. *Not-knowing is the question for all Actuals, Sami,* she'd said. *But it's a good question—to wonder who you are—because it means you have the ability to grow, change, and explore. The most important things are freedom and courage—whether you are Actual or Flicker. Never let go of your freedom or your courage, whoever you become.*

"I know," Sami said. "And never, ever give up."

Never, ever, ever, the Flicker agreed as the two of them looked up toward that very distant opening.

Sami scanned the room sleepily. It felt like things were right in the world. The sky beyond her window was so deep, the stars seemed to pop. For a moment, in fact, she thought she saw, just beside the moon, the outline of a person drifting within the night. Inside that outline, a constellation appeared to glow with blue light. And one red star.

As the night hung over the house, the memory of Ashrafieh's words shimmered all around her: *ever, ever, ever, ever.*

AUTHOR'S NOTE

Sami, the main character of Silverworld, walked into my imagination about five years ago. Like me, Sami is a child of an immigrant parent, someone who lives between cultures, between an American identity and a sense of an elusive—almost magical—old world.

On that warm spring afternoon, I was visiting my family's village outside Amman, Jordan, when I was stopped and "recognized" on the street by a total stranger, an elderly Arab man, who walked up to me and said, "Anissa?" That was my grandmother's name. This moment felt deeply mysterious to me: I'd never met my grandmother.

Anissa had lived in another country, years before I was born, yet I couldn't help wishing for a magical door that would let us find each other. Silverworld is, in part, my attempt to write that door into being, to peer between generations, countries, and realities.

Stories were Anissa's hedge against loneliness and isolation. She'd left Nazareth as a young girl. In her adopted country of Jordan, books became her refuge. She collected them, gradually amassing a library in her home. If anyone came to visit, my uncles said, Anissa would ask for a book; and she sent her guests home with books. I believe the presence of stories gave her a sense of comfort; the continuity of narrative became another kind of homeland.

My father, who immigrated to America, continued his mother's literary tradition, weaving stories for his American children about his travels around the world. He'd always assumed that his time in the States would be temporary and he tried to relocate our family to Jordan more than once. But each time he returned to his native country, he became restless and discontented: within a few months, we'd be on our way back to New York again.

I inherited a touch of this same restlessness and I sometimes refer to myself as a genetic nomad: I've traveled through much of the Middle East, to Lebanon, Syria, Egypt, Dubai, the West Bank, and the UAE. As an adult, I lived in Jordan for a year, trying it on for myself, trying to figure out where in the world to call home. Like my grandmother, I've come to believe that stories can offer an important homeland.

There's a lot of me in my character Sami—both of us torn between identities. Silverworld is the land that reflects the known world, just as, for so many of us in this country, the children of immigrants, we live between the present and the magic of faraway places and times. Up until now, I've written books, like my novel *Crescent*, and memoirs, like *The Language of Baklava*, geared toward adults. But with the birth of my daughter ten years ago, I began to feel the need to tell another kind of story. This is the book that I wish I'd had when I was her age—a journey through the experience of being in between and a celebration of the power of self-acceptance.

I hope you'll find something to connect to here as well. As book lovers, you have one of the greatest magical powers of all—the ability to travel to different worlds and to share them with others. Thank you for being my heroes.

ACKNOWLEDGMENTS

With special thanks to Phoebe Yeh and Joy Harris, who made it happen. To Andrea Gollin and Cristina Nosti, who read various versions of this book and helped me to understand it. To Scott Eason, who makes it possible.

And extra-special gratitude to the people who shared their childhood with the adult me: Jacob App, Jordan App, Lauren Bare, Grace Abujaber-Eason, Alec Effinger, and Katie Effinger. Thank you for reminding me of the importance of stories, creativity, and magic.

ABOUT THE AUTHOR

Diana Abu-Jaber has written four award-winning novels for adults: *Birds of Paradise, Origin, Crescent,* and *Arabian Jazz.* Her memoirs, *Life Without a Recipe* and *The Language of Baklava,* have been published in many languages and taught around the world. As the daughter of a Jordanian immigrant, Diana spent much of her childhood in the Middle East and especially loved listening to her relatives' folktales about the jinn and the ifrit. After her own daughter was born, Diana began weaving her a bedtime folktale that became the basis of *Silverworld.*

Diana teaches at Portland State University and lives with her family in Fort Lauderdale, Florida.

dianaabujaber.com